A man in a blue robe pushed his way through the crowd. His face was completely covered by a green goblin mask. Shoving Mrs. Wong out of the way, the man seized the pearls around Tiffany's neck. With a yank, he pulled them away from her.

"Help! Thief!" Mrs. Wong shouted.

Auntie Tiger Lil's face got an expression I had seen in a film just before she ordered somebody's head chopped off. Despite the heat inside my costume, I felt a little shiver pass up my spine. In the short time she'd been staying with us, I'd quickly learned that Auntie Tiger Lil was the one person you never crossed.

Though Auntie Tiger Lil was small, she had a voice that could carry across one of those large Hong Kong-style restaurants that are built like auditoriums.

"Come back here," Auntie shouted as she chased the thief.

"Auntie Tiger Lil. You don't have your stunt double here," I yelled as I started after her.

## ALSO BY LAURENCE YEP

Sweetwater

Dragonwings
*A 1976 Newbery Honor Book*

Child of the Owl

The Serpent's Children

Mountain Light

The Rainbow People

Tongues of Jade

Dragon's Gate
*A 1994 Newbery Honor Book*

Thief of Hearts

### DRAGON OF THE LOST SEA FANTASIES

Dragon of the Lost Sea

Dragon Steel

Dragon Cauldron

Dragon War

## EDITED BY LAURENCE YEP

American Dragons
*Twenty-Five Asian American Voices*

# LAURENCE YEP

## The Case of the

# GOBLIN PEARLS

CHINATOWN

Mystery
#1

📖 HarperTrophy®
*A Division of HarperCollinsPublishers*

The Case of the Goblin Pearls
Copyright © 1997 by Laurence Yep
All rights reserved. No part of this book may be used or reproduced in any manner
whatsoever without written permission except in the case of brief
quotations embodied in critical articles and reviews.
Printed in the United States of America. For information address
HarperCollins Children's Books, a division of HarperCollins Publishers,
10 East 53rd Street, New York, NY 10022.

Library of Congress Cataloging-in-Publication Data
Yep, Laurence.
    The case of the Goblin Pearls / Laurence Yep.
        p.      cm. — (Chinatown ; 1)
    Summary: Lily and her aunt, a Chinese American movie actress, join forces to solve the
theft of some priceless pearls and stop the operator of a sweatshop in San Francisco's
Chinatown.
    ISBN 0-06-024444-5. — ISBN 0-06-024446-1 (lib. bdg.)
    ISBN 0-06-440552-4 (pbk.)
    [1. Mystery and detective stories.    2. Chinese Americans—Fiction.    3. Chinatown
(San Francisco, Calif.)—Fiction.]    I. Title.    II. Series: Yep, Laurence.    Chinatown ; 1.
PZ7.Y44Cas    1997                                                                  96-22924
[Fic]—dc20                                                                                CIP
                                                                                            AC

Typography by Al Cetta
❖
First Harper Trophy edition, 1998

Visit us on the World Wide Web!
http://www.harperchildrens.com

TO ALL MY AUNTIES IN AND OUT OF CHINATOWN

"Chinatown is a state of mind."

I wrote those words some nineteen years ago in *Child of the Owl*. At the time, I had already seen some of the impact that the 1965 immigration laws had upon Chinese America. Since then, I have seen the original Chinatown spill over its traditional borders in San Francisco just as the Chinatowns in New York and other urban areas have done. New enclaves have also sprung up.

And yet I think every Chinese American carries Chinatown within him or her, for Chinatown was never just a set of geographical boundaries. Chinatown is the beat of the lion drums pulsing in the blood. Chinatown is the maze of shadows as the sunlight struggles through rooftop antennas and fire escapes. Chinatown is the treasure chest when a grandmother opens a kitchen cupboard. Chinatown is sunlit asphalt; a river of sounds; a cool, gray sanctuary. It is a sigh, a smell, a tear, a laugh.

So these books about Auntie Tiger Lil are an attempt to define what I like most and least in Chinatown. Especially that Chinatown within the heart.

Though Tiger Lil is fictitious, she is based on a number of my mother's friends, all of them funny, strong women. And though Happy Fortune is also invented, unfortunately the working conditions are not. It is a shameful, ongoing abuse.

# CHAPTER ONE

Though Chinese New Year was a month away, kids had already begun setting off firecrackers. I heard the sharp *pop-pop-pop* in the distance down the hill in Chinatown. My parents had told me that firecrackers helped scare away the goblins and evil spirits, and though it was early, I suppose some people figured they might as well start now. The way people complained about Chinatown, its streets and alleys were full of goblins. Literally.

Dad came home with the news. "Mrs. Sung got mugged this morning."

"That sweet little old lady?" I wondered.

"She'd just bought her groceries in Chinatown and was on her way home," Dad said. "She's walked that route safely for thirty years. It was that same bunch of kids in Chinese opera spirit masks. They call themselves the Powell Street Boys."

"What's she going to do now?" Mom asked.

"Her kids have given her money to take taxicabs," he said.

"Good luck getting a taxi to come into Chinatown to take her just a few blocks," Mom said. "They say the traffic's too congested and trips take too long."

As I listened to the distant firecrackers, I thought I could have used some firepower myself. Some goblin was spoiling the loop routine in my computer program. I could have called up some of the others in my homework group, but the only one who knew anything was Akeem, and I didn't want to call *him*.

I was deep in the problem when the phone rang, so I didn't answer.

Mom's voice floated down the hallway from the kitchen. "Lily, will you get that?"

"I'm busy, Mom," I shouted back, annoyed.

"Chris?" Mom called to my older brother.

"Busy," he yelled.

With a loud sigh, Mom stomped into the hallway and answered the telephone. Her crankiness evaporated as soon as she recognized the caller. "Auntie Tiger Lil, what a pleasant surprise." And a second later she began squealing in a high-pitched voice like one of those quiz-show contestants when they win a big prize. "What? No? Really?"

Curiosity drew me where duty couldn't, and I went to the doorway of my bedroom. Mom had gotten so carried away that she was hopping around. "Sure, you can stay with us. No, I know Henry would say the same thing."

Henry was my dad, who designed computer chips in Silicon Valley south of San Francisco. My mom, Mabel, had a beauty shop.

"When should we expect you?" Mom asked. "In a week? Great. And don't you worry about a thing."

Usually I'm the doormat in the family, afraid to say anything. If there's extra chores to be done, it's me who does them. And if we have relatives visit, it's me who gives up her room and sleeps on the sofa. So as soon as Mom hung up, I said, "I'll move my stuff, Mom."

Mom opened a drawer in the telephone stand. "Thank you, dear, but I think this time you can keep your room. Your dad will give up his study."

Dad's study was the holy of holies. "The study with his computer?" I gasped.

"That's right." Mom rummaged around until she got a notepad and pen.

Foreseeing future arguments, I felt compelled to point out, "The study also has the forty-inch television and the stereo hi-fi VCR. Where are you going to put those?"

"The Forty-Niners aren't in the postseason games. He won't miss it, and Auntie can watch movies." Mom calmly began to write a list of things to do. "A big star like Auntie will need to keep up on what's current in show biz."

Auntie Tiger Lil might have been an astronaut living on the moon for all I really knew about her. Every Christmas and every birthday she sent expensive gifts by

3

mail from Beverly Hills—but sometimes in her careless-
ness she left the price tags on.

"If she's such a big star, why's she staying here?" I
wondered. "She's rich. She could afford a hotel."

"Of course she could," Mom replied. "But she's also
family, so our door's always open to her. Besides, she has
to be up here until New Year's. She's arranging an entire
float and parade unit."

Mom was excited as a little kid about Auntie's coming to stay. I couldn't help asking, "This is what's always
puzzled me, Mom. If Auntie's so famous, how come
Chris and I have never seen any of her movies?"

"She made movies with Fred MacMurray, Alan
Ladd, Maureen O'Hara and a whole bunch of other
stars." And she rattled off another half dozen names I'd
never heard of.

"Are they pretty famous?" I asked.

Mom stiffened. "Of course. And they can act rings
around the film punks you like."

Personally I had my doubts, but I knew better than
to get Mom worked up. "Were they silent movies? Or
did they have sound?"

"That's it. I am going to go to the video store and
rent Auntie's movies for you to see." And she added yet
another item to the bottom of her list.

So that was how we began the Tiger Lil film festival
that evening in Dad's study. Mom started out with an
old musical, *Make Mine Mink*, from the fifties starring
somebody called Doris Day.

4

Chris was a taller version of my dad—as if someone had taken Dad and stretched him like taffy. Maybe they were too much alike, because they were always arguing—especially since Chris had started high school. Almost every evening, he egged Dad into a fight.

At that moment, Chris rested the edge of his palm across his forehead as he scanned the film credits rolling across Dad's big screen. "Where's Auntie?"

For once, though, Dad refused to rise to the bait. Instead, he kicked back in his recliner. "She's coming up."

To my surprise, Dad had taken the temporary loss of his study very well. As he stared eagerly at the screen, I thought he was even thrilled that Auntie was going to inhabit his study. "There," he said, hitting the pause button on his remote.

The introductory music suddenly stopped, and frozen on the screen was a list of twelve names. The typeface was so small that it was a good thing we were watching it on a big screen. Sure enough, there was Lily Leung.

"This is before she began the Tiger Lil series," Mom explained.

I was puzzled. "Like a television series?"

Mom started the movie again. "No. Back in the glory days of Hollywood, they would do a whole string of movies built around a character. There was *The Thin Man* with William Powell, Ann Sothern in the Maisie movies. They used to show them on TV later on."

"Like the Rocky movies."

Chris looked at me and I just rolled my eyes. Most of the movie dragged on until we saw the Chinese maid help Doris Day take off her fur stole after a night on the town.

"She's just a maid," Chris hooted.

"Quiet," Mom snapped.

In the movie, Auntie was shaking her head. "Don't you ever get tired of making all those poor little minks run around naked?"

As Doris Day made some reply, I couldn't help frowning. "Fur coats are nothing to joke about."

I guess Jupiter, Mars and Venus must have all been in alignment, because for once Chris agreed with me. "That's right."

"Shh," Dad said.

On the screen, Auntie was hanging the coat up in a closet. "Well, I can't help it," she was saying. "You're not the one who has to go inside the closet and see all these beady little eyes staring at you accusingly."

Mom laughed, and Dad roared as he slapped a chair arm. "She always gets the best lines."

When the heroine glared, Auntie did a little dance step that Mom called a buck and wing.

As the camera focused in on the blond heroine again, Mom turned to Dad. "Maybe we ought to go on to the next one, Henry. I think the children are getting bored." She pointed to another tape. "Try *Babes in Baghdad*."

"Don't you want to see Auntie some more in this one?" I asked.

Mom shrugged. "That was Auntie's only scene."

The trouble was that Auntie usually had only one scene in the next ones too. She was funny, but she didn't have much time on camera, and she almost always seemed to be a maid. "What about the Tiger Lil series?" I wondered.

While a tape rewound, Mom confessed, "I'm sorry, dear. I tried every video store in San Francisco, and no one has any of the Tiger Lil films."

"It must have something to do with the rights," Dad said, trying to explain it away.

Next to me, Chris had been squirming all this time, so I was ready for the explosion. "Maybe it's because they're not very good."

Mom and Dad stared at Chris as if they'd suddenly found a monster in their midst.

"You watch your tongue," Dad growled.

Mom drew herself up indignantly. "Auntie is a fabulous actor."

Chris spread his hands. "She only plays servants. If she were a man, she'd be playing houseboys."

Mom ticked off the items on her fingers. "She's a tough, funny, independent woman—like Joan Blondell and Eve Arden and Ann Sothern."

"What they would have called a 'brassy broad,'" Dad chimed in.

Chris and I exchanged looks about the strange

names, which neither of us recognized. I risked provoking Mom. "Is that what the character of Tiger Lil was like?"

Mom brightened. She picked up an old scrapbook from the coffee table. "You can read the reviews yourself. I dug it out of the closet this afternoon."

Mom began turning the brittle, yellow pages. There were eight-by-ten publicity shots in black and white, but there were also glamour spreads from fan magazines—all of them in old hair fashions and clothing styles. "My grandmother started it; but when she died, I kept it up," she said.

As she and Dad took turns reading the reviews out loud, they seemed to forget about us. I could hear the pride they took in Auntie's good reviews, but they might as well have been talking about Martians for all I knew. And yet they seemed to think I should care. I felt creepy, the way I did when my uncle Eddy tried to talk about the Vietnam war. He would mention names but never explain who they were—just this long list of the dead or dying.

While they reminisced, I looked over their bowed heads at Chris. Silently his lips shaped the word "Pa-the-tic."

# CHAPTER TWO

Chris and I excused ourselves as soon as we could. In a short time, I could hear his small television through the door to his room, but I felt sorry for my folks. I couldn't shake that sense of pity. And maybe I was just a little curious, too.

Risking the wrath of Akeem, I dialed him on my telephone extension. Before I could even say hello, he grumped, "Don't bother me."

"Oh, sorry," I said, "but this is important."

He must have recognized my voice, because he simply grumbled, "I haven't finished our computer program, and I never will if you keep interrupting me."

"Please don't hang up!" I begged.

I think he would have hung up anyway on most everyone else, but he had a soft spot for me—such as it was. "What is it you want, Lily?" he demanded.

"Why do you think I want something?" I said.

"Because," Akeem observed, "no one calls me for

fun." He said it calmly, as if he were talking about the weather.

"Okay," I said, admitting the truth of that. "I was wondering if you could help me track down any of the Tiger Lil films." I explained about Auntie.

On the other end of the line, Akeem complained, "What do you think I am? Your local video store?"

To obtain Akeem's help, you had to appeal to his pride. "My mother's tried every video store in San Francisco, and she hasn't been able to find any of my great-aunt's movies. She's coming to visit us for a while, so I thought it'd be nice to know what she's done. I thought with your connections on the Internet, you might be able to locate some videotape copies. You're my last hope."

"Hmm," he said as he considered the problem. "Do you know the film titles?" After I had told him as many as I could remember from the reviews, he said, "She sounds interesting. I'll get back to you. Don't bother me in the meantime."

An hour later, he called back. "Well, it wasn't easy," he said, and paused, waiting for me to stroke his ego.

"I knew you could do it," I said.

He grunted. "Of course, but it took a little hunting. You'll find the film titles at a video store over in Berkeley." And he gave me the name.

"Thanks. I owe you," I said.

A couple of times we had partnered on English projects—mostly because I was the only one in the class who would. Akeem had little patience with people who didn't understand everything he did, and most people didn't.

"And you can bet I'll collect," he said, and hung up quickly before I could ask for anything more.

Mom was thrilled when I gave her the name of the store, but she blanched when she heard it was in Berkeley. "Isn't there anything closer?"

I fixed the Post-it with the information to the back of her hand. "Sorry, Mom. You'll just have to take BART." BART was the local subway, and her fear of it had become a family joke. Though we had a car, Mom refused to drive over the Bay Bridge since it had collapsed in the last Earthquake.

She shivered. "But the BART tubes go under the bay. What if there's an earthquake?"

"Would Uncle Jackie build something that wasn't safe?" Dad teased her. Uncle Jackie was an engineer who had worked on building the BART tubes.

Mom detached the Post-it. "Not intentionally." Mom considered the matter unhappily and then drew back her shoulders. "Well, I guess it'll have to do."

If I thought the matter ended there, I was wrong. Auntie's visit was like a pebble thrown into a pond— only as the ripples spread out, they got bigger instead of weaker.

The next day at school, I was in the computer lab when Akeem sat down next to me. "Well?" he asked, giving me a nudge.

I jabbed back with my elbow. "Well, what?"

"When is your great-aunt coming?" Akeem said.

Akeem's friend Barry leaned over and whispered something into Akeem's ear before he sat down on Akeem's right. Barry looked Caucasian except for the epicanthic folds on his eyes. Akeem did most of the talking for them, because Barry always seemed to walk around with a perpetual chip on his shoulder.

They were an odd combination, since Akeem was as crazy about computers as Barry was about the martial arts. They'd become buddies because of a shared passion for one bloody computer game that any decent human being would detest.

"We'd like to meet her," Akeem said.

Up to now, Akeem and Barry had made me feel like I was so much driftwood on our computer team. "What for?"

Akeem put a hand over the monitor screen so I couldn't ignore them. "She's made a lot of movies."

"Who's made a lot of movies?" Ariadne asked. She was a tall brunette with a long, graceful neck. Her father lived in Paris, but her mother lived in an expensive condo in Pacific Heights with a beautiful view of the bay and the Marin headlands beyond. Bright and funny, she was easily the most popular girl in school.

Though Ms. Tucker, the computer lab teacher, called us a team, we were anything but that. Akeem and I tolerated one another out of mutual interest in school-work. Barry put up with me because of Akeem. And

Ariadne had attached herself to the team because any group with Akeem was likely to get an A in computer lab. Other than computer lab, we went our own separate ways: Akeem and Barry in their hacker world, Ariadne in high society. They were all doers and achievers. Me? I just went spinning along in the shadows, afraid to try anything.

Akeem held up a disk in his spare hand. "Lily's great-aunt made dozens of movies. I looked it up."

It seemed strange to have everyone paying attention to me—even if it was because of Auntie. Usually they took me for granted—like a desk or a chair. I wasn't sure I liked it.

I shoved Akeem's hand away from the screen. "We don't have time for this. What about the assignment?" I asked. "It's due next week."

"I'll handle it. Don't I always?" Akeem reached over my arms to poke at the keyboard. Once he'd quit the assignment, he put in the other disk and called up the filmography. "This is only a partial list."

Ariadne and Barry leaned in to stare at the screen. As the titles rolled past, I watched them shake their heads.

"Nope. Never heard of any of these," Ariadne finally said.

For a moment, I wished I had Mom's scrapbook; but then I realized that the faded yellow clippings would not impress them any more than they had me.

I felt my cheeks reddening with embarrassment

13

until Akeem glanced at me. "Must be a pretty lame career," he said.

Usually I try to avoid trouble, so I keep my mouth shut; but his arrogance got my goat. "What was the last movie you saw?" I demanded. "I mean a real movie—one that didn't have a hero with pecs bigger than his girlfriend?"

As Barry whispered to Akeem, I added, "One where a car didn't blow up."

That stumped them, and I couldn't help going on to brag. "Auntie Lil even made a movie with Clark Gable."

Akeem's and Barry's faces were as blank as mine had been when I'd heard that name, but Ariadne's face lit up. "Really?"

"You've heard of him?" Barry asked.

Ariadne dropped her eyes sadly. "While my grandmother was alive, she lived with me and my mom. She was a sick a lot, so we used to watch old movies together. She used to sew in the garment district back in New York."

It was the first hint to me that Ariadne had ever led anything less than a perfect life. It made me feel closer to her in a way.

Barry whispered to Akeem, who cracked his knuckles the way he did before he tackled the keyboard. "Why don't we rent some of her movies? We've got the list."

In a panic, I realized what my bragging had done. What if they went out and saw the movies I had?

Instead of being impressed, they would know I'd just been trying to puff myself up along with my great-aunt. Grabbing the keyboard, I hastily closed the file. "Let's get back to work before Tucker catches us."

For the rest of the lab, we worked on the project; and as soon as the bell rang, I bolted out of the room.

The last thing I wanted to hear when I got home was Auntie's name. But imagine my surprise that evening when Mom produced three movies for us to watch. "I closed up the beauty parlor and headed over on BART."

I stared at her in amazement.

She sighed as if she didn't believe her good fortune. "Fortunately there wasn't any earthquake, and the tubes under the bay didn't crack." I guess the tapes were really important to my mother.

I picked up the first movie in its worn cardboard carton. It was *Hold That Tiger Lil*. Swiftly I ran my eye down the titles on the spines of the other two. They were both Tiger Lil films too: *Watch Out, Tiger Lil* and *Tiger Lil to the Rescue*. "You shouldn't have rented all of these, Mom. We can't watch them all tonight."

"I bought them," she announced triumphantly. "And if they'd had all the Tiger Lil films, I would have bought them too. It wasn't cheap, but it's time you kids know your heritage."

Mom said that she would show them in sequence, and so that night I sat down prepared to humor her even if I dropped dead of boredom. Chris, though, wouldn't watch. "I refuse to see more cultural stereotypes. We're still surrounded by them."

I knew how much they meant to Mom, though, so I whispered to him, "How can you complain about the series without seeing it?"

Chris scratched one ear and then the other. "I suppose I could manage to watch a few."

However, as soon as the first movie, *Hold That Tiger Lil*, began on the screen, I started to enjoy myself.

Auntie Tiger Lil still played the same kind of role—the "brassy broad"—that we had seen the other night, but now she was the center of the movie. She was a wisecracking chorus girl who'd inherited a greasy-spoon restaurant from an old boyfriend. When some gangsters tried to extort protection money, she stood her ground and took them all on.

It was great to see an Asian—especially an Asian woman—taking the lead. I found myself laughing and crying at the right moments. And when Tiger Lil had her back to the roof's edge and was surrounded by the gangsters, I sat on the edge of my seat.

Auntie turned, then, and looked directly at the camera. "What the heck?" she said with a shrug. Turning, she jumped over an alley to the next roof.

I started to cheer as she made her escape across the rooftops, and Mom and Dad started to clap.

I was surprised, though, when the movie finished in little over an hour. "That was short—thank Heaven," Chris observed.

16

"Let's see another," I suggested eagerly.

"You'd almost think you enjoyed them," Mom said, trying to hide how pleased she was.

And Auntie only got better with each movie: funnier, sharper, more resourceful. In *Watch Out, Tiger Lil*, Auntie took a job as a secretary in an office, not realizing it was a front for a bunch of spies. And in *Tiger Lil to the Rescue*, Tiger Lil was the only one on a jury who believed the defendant was innocent and set out to prove it.

By the time we'd finished the third movie, I thought that here were movies I could show the team and not be embarrassed.

As Dad snapped on the lights and began to rewind the tape, he looked at Chris and me. "Well, what'd you think?"

"She was great." I put my hand on the trio of videos. "Can I lend these to some of the kids at school?"

Chris, though, drew himself up in his most self-righteous pose. "Why? She's just a parody of a Chinese. She plays the roles whites want to see a Chinese in, not the way we really are."

I dug an elbow into his side. "I didn't think she was that bad. In fact, I thought she was pretty strong." I was sure Ariadne, at least, would enjoy her, and the story moved fast enough and had enough wisecracks to probably please Akeem and Barry.

Mom loyally clutched a videotape of Auntie. "The early movies were the only roles she could get back

17

then. And eventually she got to play Tiger Lil. And that was a role model we could look up to as kids. We didn't have others."

Dad wagged a finger at Chris. "So you show your great-aunt some respect. She belongs to a generation that fought a lot of battles for those of us who came later, including you."

Chris' shoulders grew rigid. You'd have thought Dad would have learned by now. Chris automatically did anything he was told not to do and disagreed with everything.

Mom, though, was more diplomatic—and effective. She put a hand on Chris' arm. "She's always been a special person in my life, Chris. So even if you can't show respect, can you keep quiet?"

Chris' head dipped reluctantly. "All right," he mumbled. Shoving himself up from the couch, he shambled off.

Because of Chris' fuming, I debated the next day whether to bring the videotapes to school or not. Would the other kids laugh? That was my trouble: I was always afraid to do anything because someone might laugh. So for once I decided to do something.

Snagging the three tapes, I parceled them out to my teammates. Just in case they thought they were lame, I covered myself by warning them they were pretty old.

However, that evening, Ariadne herself called me up to tell me my great-aunt was "fabulous." And the next day, Akeem declared her to be "cool." And even

18

Barry, through the medium of Akeem, announced my aunt was "funny."

It made me feel good to know that I had something in common with my schoolmates besides school assignments. As the others swapped movies, we enthusiastically shared favorite scenes from the movies. We were beginning to sound like friends.

So I found it easy to help my folks to redecorate Dad's study in preparation for Auntie. We plastered the walls with publicity photos and posters, and over the door Mom had fashioned a theater marquee from cardboard. In big, broad letters, she'd written, "Welcome, Tiger Lil." Beneath it, Mom had put a plastic Oscar she had bought.

Chris swaggered by in time to sneer at the marquee Dad was embellishing, outlining the letters in little Christmas lights that blinked on and off. "Do you think the shrine will make her forget?"

"Forget what?" I demanded. I was pretty proud of our work.

"She's used to mansions in Beverly Hills, nitwit," he said, scowling, "not the way we live."

Dad bristled. "We live pretty good."

"We live like scared rabbits," Chris snapped. "Didn't you hear the news? The Powell Street Boys have worked their way up from little old people. Last night they went into the Golden Wok and robbed everyone at gunpoint—the customers and the staff as well as emptying out the cash register."

"The police will catch them soon," Dad said, going back to work on the shrine.

But now that I looked at the shrine again, it did seem amateurish compared to the elaborate Hollywood sets Auntie would be used to. In fact, our whole house would seem shabby compared to the mansions in Beverly Hills. I wouldn't blame her if she turned right around and went home.

# CHAPTER THREE

The firecrackers were going off again when Auntie arrived a week later. Some far away were faint snaps, while the closer ones were loud bangs that late afternoon. I knew that there were more goblins around than usual.

Among other things, Chinatown was suffering from health problems. In the mail that afternoon, we had received a notice about tuberculosis tests. We'd already had ours, but it seemed there were a lot of newcomers who hadn't. Two cases had been reported in Chinatown, and there were fears that there would be more. Many of the newcomers could get only the poorest-paying jobs with no health care. As a result, they just got sicker until their families could not ignore the disease any longer and brought them in to the public health authorities.

Worse though, that masked gang, the Powell Street Boys, had grown bolder. The Powell Street Boys had continued robbing restaurants in Chinatown until everyone was terrified to go into them anymore.

And just this afternoon the Powell Street Boys had backed a stolen car right through the window of the biggest jewelry store in Chinatown. Smashing glass counters, they had swiftly filled their sacks with jewelry and gold and then fled before the police could arrive. Nobody knew where the Powell Street Boys would strike next.

Suddenly the firecrackers stopped. The air, though not especially hot, was humid and uncomfortable. I kept feeling like I wanted to dry myself with a towel. Because of Auntie's parade project, we'd taken an interest in the long-range weather forecast, and unfortunately the rest of the month was supposed to be wet and full of thunderstorms.

In the silence, I thought of the calm before a storm or tidal wave or some other force of nature ripped through a town.

My gloom, though, flew right out the window when a big white stretch limousine pulled up before our house.

"Jeez," I wheezed, pressing my nose against the glass, "it's big as a boat."

Chris let out a low whistle. "I guess if you have to sell out, you might as well sell out big."

A young woman in a suit and tie and gray cap got out and circled around the car to open the curbside passenger door.

On the opposite side of the street, our neighbors

22

appeared at their windows, craning their necks to see who the V.I.P. was. I wanted to shout to them that it was my famous great-aunt who was a big star in Hollywood.

I had been expecting a young woman in an evening gown and fur stoles, like in her movies. Instead, I saw a plump woman in her sixties, her face hidden by big dark glasses. She wasn't dressed glamorously, but she showed taste with a pastel mint suit and matching hat. I assumed they came from some expensive store in Beverly Hills.

As the limo driver put her two big suitcases onto the sidewalk, Auntie planted a fist on either hip and grinned. "So how's my favorite niece?" she called from the sidewalk, projecting her voice easily up two stories to where we were peering out of the living room window.

Her voice was even louder once she was inside. "And how's my favorite nephew-in-law?"

Dad gave her a hug. "Fine, Auntie. How're you doing?"

"Great, kiddo," Auntie said as he took her suitcases. "Oliver and Wayne were so apologetic that they couldn't use me in *The Joy Luck Club* that they promised to build a movie all around me. Amy just has to write the script."

Mom was leaning half over the hallway railing, as excited as a little kid. "Really, Auntie? I wondered why you weren't in it."

Auntie winked up at Mom. "Politics, Mabel. I had

the best audition, but the money people couldn't forget I was Tiger Lil."

Dad sighed heavily. "Typecast."

As I watched the elegant woman climb the steps, I began to feel ashamed. Our house must seem shabby compared to the mansions of Beverly Hills.

At the top of the stairs, Auntie surveyed Chris. "And who's this good-looking lug?"

"This is our son, Chris," Mom said, putting her hands on Chris' arms.

I said a silent prayer that Chris would behave himself, but Auntie's grand arrival seemed to have stunned him. Mutely, he held out his hand.

Auntie cupped his chin and positioned his head at various angles, grunting with satisfaction each time she did. "We'll get some head shots taken, kiddo, and I'll start circulating them among the casting agents."

"Oh, no, you don't." Dad puffed as he set her bags on the landing. "He's going to become an engineer."

Auntie released Chris with a sigh. "What a waste. He's got your good bones, Henry."

"Actually, I'm going into poli sci," Chris mumbled shyly.

Dad glared. "Engineering."

Auntie sized up the situation in a glance. Slipping between them, she hooked an arm through Dad's. "Now, Henry, he's handsome enough to be a Kennedy."

Chris looked at Auntie gratefully, and I could see

she'd won points with him. Dad, though, snorted. "Politics is a disease, not a profession."

Before Chris could defend his choice, Mom sprang in. "And this is your namesake, Auntie." She switched her hands to my shoulders.

"Pleased to meet you," I said. Auntie had so much energy that now I knew how Dorothy must have felt when the tornado was taking her to Oz.

Mom was pretty in a normal sort of way, but though Auntie was in her sixties, you could still see that Tiger Lil had once been beautiful enough to be in motion pictures. "And I'm so pleased to meet you finally," she said to me.

Mom took Auntie's arm. "Come on, Auntie. We want to show you your room."

"Wait, wait." Dad jogged down the hallway. The next moment he had turned on the marquee so that the lights began flashing on and off.

When she saw it, Auntie clapped her hands together. "I won't be more pleased when I get my star on Hollywood Boulevard."

I had seen newscasts of celebrities getting a star on a piece of pavement. "You're getting a star?"

Auntie's eyes lingered wistfully on the marquee. "As soon as they finish making repairs to the street."

"It's about time," Dad said with a firm nod.

Auntie, though, seemed calm enough about being ignored by the film industry. "Pooh, who has time for worrying about those things?"

With a little prompting, Auntie began talking about all her various projects, dropping names that I recognized from the newspapers. Mom and Dad just drank it up like sponges. Even Chris hovered nearby, listening.

"I guess you're going to get pretty bored up here," I finally said, apologetically. "I mean, there won't be any of your famous friends around or any Hollywood premieres."

"Everyone needs a rest from the hustle and bustle," Auntie said, kissing me on the cheek. "A little peace and quiet will be just the thing I need, so I was glad to help out Mr. Soo."

"Which Mr. Soo?" Dad asked. "The principal?"

"No. This Mr. Soo comes from Hong Kong. He makes a medicinal cure called Lion Salve," Auntie said as she set down her purse and began to unbutton her coat.

Dad let out a low whistle. "It's second only to Tiger Balm in sales."

Auntie held out her hands, and it took me a moment to realize she wanted me to help her out of her coat. "He's decided it's time Americans had the benefit of our medicine. And he asked me to help him draw up the publicity campaign. It was my idea to introduce his product to America at the Chinese New Year's parade. Mr. Soo wants me to arrange a float in the parade and then a reception afterward. And since I happen to know a number of professionals who build floats for the Rose

26

Parade, I decided to have some fun. So I got them to come up here. They're in a hotel, but I wanted to visit my family too."

"You'd be great at publicity, Auntie," Mom said. "Maybe you should even take it up as a sideline."

"Do you really think so?" Auntie asked coyly.

When we all agreed dutifully with Mom, Auntie picked up her purse again, fishing out pieces of paper. "Fax these costume sketches to this number, kiddo." When she unfolded them, I saw the costumes looked like large jars.

"We don't have a fax machine," I said.

"Go next door to Mr. Li," Mom suggested.

Auntie stopped me. "Wait, I'll have more faxes. Might as well do them all at once." She whirled around to Mom. "Mabel, I need local actors, too, so I'll have to place ads in the major papers for auditions."

"What do you want the ads to say?" Mom asked, a little dazed.

"You think it up." Auntie added, "But show it to me first before you call it in. Henry, call up the local talent agencies and explain what I want."

Dad looked just as stunned as the rest of us. "Yes, Auntie."

Auntie began hunting in her purse for something. "And I've got to find some warehouse space close enough to Chinatown."

"They don't send the parade down Grant Avenue anymore, Auntie," Dad informed her. "The fire marshals said the streets are too narrow. I think they begin now south of Market."

Auntie yanked some small keys from her purse. "Somewhere in my bags is an information packet that the parade committee sent me. These should open the locks."

The overstuffed bag seemed almost to explode when Auntie undid the locks. Blouses and scarves and sweaters poured out of the abused luggage. Digging through the piles, Auntie found a thick green folder and handed it to Dad. "Think you can handle it, Henry?"

Dad hefted the folder but managed a smile. "It'll be good practice for when the company moves me up to the managerial level."

She assigned a job to each of us before she called her boss, Mr. Soo. "What?" she said. "Where's the television?" she asked me.

"The nearest is in your room," Mom said.

"Hold on," Auntie said to Mr. Soo. Setting the phone down, Auntie entered the "shrine" and hastily turned on the television.

"This afternoon, Supervisor Macek called upon the mayor and his fellow supervisors to do something about crime in Chinatown," the announcer intoned solemnly. The station cut to footage of a middle-aged man with a bad toupee holding up a newspaper to the camera. The headline, in huge type, screamed, "Big Chinatown Heist."

"Since the police cannot seem to defend Chinatown against this band of hooligans, how can they protect the hundreds of thousands of visitors who will come into Chinatown before and after the parade? The answer is simple: They can't. So I am going to make a proposal that this year the parade be canceled."

Auntie rocked back on her heels. "He can't do that."

Dad dismissed the supervisor with a wave of his hand. "He's just trying to weasel his way into the mayor's office. His real target is the police chief, who's the mayor's buddy. He's trying to make the police chief seem incompetent."

Auntie picked up Dad's argument. "Right, ambitious . . . police chief . . . incompetent." The next moment she had run out into the hall and was trying to reassure Mr. Soo. "No, he's just a political hack . . ." she was saying.

Mom sighed. "It doesn't matter whether he cancels the parade or not. That kind of talk will keep the tourists away from Chinatown."

"It's fake Chinese culture anyway," Chris said with his nose in the air.

The news anchor came back on. "And in a related story, the wealthy H. T. Wong, well known in San Francisco society, has thrown down the gauntlet to the Powell Street Boys." The next moment the television screen was filled with the image of a woman whose hair was a globe of black curls. Around her neck was a thick rope of white spheres. They looked like pearls, but they were so large—the size of mothballs—that I figured they couldn't be.

"Auntie," I shouted. "You'd better come in here."

Auntie poked her head through the doorway. "That's Mrs. Wong."

"Who's she?" I asked.

Dad watched the screen intently. "She and her husband own a good chunk of Chinatown as well as a ritzy apartment house in Pacific Heights." That was one of the expensive neighborhoods in San Francisco.

In the meantime, Mrs. Wong began to say in a crisp, posh accent, "My husband and I came to America as poor immigrants. We believe in the American dream and in American justice. As a symbol of that faith, my daughter will wear the Goblin Pearls when she rides in the New Year's parade. We know that she will be as safe as in our own home." She shook her fist at the camera. "We Chinese will not be bullied by a bunch of hoodlums."

Mom shook her head. "I never thought Mrs. Wong would be so civic-minded."

The anchor came back on. "The Goblin Pearls are ancient, almost priceless. Legend says that they originally belonged to three goblins named Greed, Pride and Desire. However, a poet named Li Ho stole them and presented them to his girlfriend. When the goblins tracked him down, he fought them long enough to let his girlfriend get away with the necklace. So the frustrated goblins took him instead. No one ever saw him again, and it is said the goblins are still trying to get their pearls back. It's said that the pearls bring nothing but bad luck. Let's hope this brave woman doesn't have real goblins coming after her."

"The pearls are pure bad luck," Dad swore.

"Mrs. Wong isn't helping any by flaunting them in the faces of the Powell Street Boys," Mom said.

"She's got more guts than the rest of us," Dad said.

"Guts or not, there's one thing I don't understand. Pearls like that are a cultural treasure in China," Chris said. "How did she ever get them to America?"

"She probably bought the right papers." Dad shrugged.

Auntie groaned. "And her daughter's on my float. Mr. Soo picked her to be his Miss Lion Salve." Putting a hand to her head, she ran back into the hallway to reassure Mr. Soo about the latest challenge.

# CHAPTER FOUR

For the next few days, I never knew what I'd find when I got home. Sometimes Auntie was meeting with Chinatown bigwigs to make sure the parade got held—bankers and merchants and political activist groups like the Chinese American Citizens Alliance.

The star, though, was Mrs. Wong. I thought for sure that there'd be some black thundercloud trailing behind her with lightning ready to strike. The first time the group met, she got a standing ovation.

"We thought we'd get to see the Goblin Pearls," a banker said.

Mrs. Wong patted her hair, flustered and flattered by the applause. "We have to save them for the main event."

"Aren't you afraid?" a jeweler asked. "I hear there's a curse on them."

"That's just the story that came with them." Mrs. Wong chuckled. "But of course that's all superstition."

The others laughed with her, but some looked more nervous than others. And I noticed that at the next meeting, no one sat close to her except Auntie.

I think Auntie was too busy to be scared of anything. When she wasn't arranging protest meetings, she was hiring and rehearsing actors, getting costumes ordered and having a float built. And yet somehow Auntie still found time to make our lives seem like Halloween, New Year's and Christmas all rolled up into one. One night she catered a romantic dinner for our parents, complete with a Gypsy violinist. The next evening it was a marbles tournament with an old sock as a prize. The evening after that it was a hermit crab race. At sixty plus, she had more energy than I did, and I was only twelve.

Everything had to be an "event"—I guess because she had a natural talent for organizing things. She had friends from Hollywood all over the city. "Did they all move up here in one big group?" I asked her.

"Well, they're not just actors. Some are hair stylists or costumers or electricians and carpenters. And they all have skills they can use elsewhere. Now, I've made a lot of movies, and I always make it a point to get to know the crews. And when they got out of show biz, I kept in touch with them. They're spread all across the country."

"That's some network," I said, whistling.

In fact, she seemed less and less like a guest, and more like some entertainment director on a cruise ship. If she wasn't managing some event, she always had some funny story to tell or some scene to act out. She could make even a chapter from *Silas Marner* seem funny.

However, even in the midst of laughing, I felt twinges of embarrassment. The more she organized, the more I was sure our house and lives seemed shabby to her. All her "events" seemed a quiet comment on how boring we were.

Of course, the more I told my teammates about my great-aunt's shenanigans, the more they wanted to know.

Finally one day they trooped into the computer lab as a group and sat down around me in a circle.

"We want to meet your great-aunt," Ariadne announced.

"I, too, would like to meet your famous aunt," Linda Chin said from the next table. She was a tall girl with a ponytail.

I blinked, because it was the first time I had ever heard Linda speak except in class. However, she picked a fine time to assert herself.

I had to look up slightly at Linda. "My great-aunt's too busy with a big project for the New Year's parade."

"Oh, I see," Linda said. It was hard to read her reaction.

"Can you imagine the nerve? Eavesdropping," Ariadne said in a voice loud enough for Linda to overhear.

I motioned for Ariadne to speak lower, but Akeem chimed in. "What a mooch. She never has any money. She's always borrowing magazines or books from people."

I think that was the opinion of most of the kids in the school.

Through Akeem, Barry added, "You never see her at after-school activities."

"Yeah, she never goes to dances," Ariadne said, as if that were a criminal offense.

"And not to movies, not to anything," Akeem finished off.

"It's like she lives in a separate dimension after school," Barry agreed.

Ariadne hummed the theme from *The Twilight Zone*. "No one's ever been to her home. Do you think she's an alien?"

"So she's a drudge." I shrugged. In fact, there was a faint whiff of airplane fuel to her—as in J.O.J., or Just Off the Jet. You couldn't expect a J.O.J. to understand the proper way to do things.

Ariadne got back to business. "So what about your great-aunt?"

"I've got to check with her to see if it's okay," I said. "I'll tell you tomorrow."

"But I can't wait any longer," Ariadne complained.

Fortunately, the bell rang beginning the lab, and everyone got down to business. And when I got home after school, I tried to ask Auntie, but she was busy on the telephone.

The problem, though, with dealing with doers like Akeem and Ariadne was that they refused to wait. I suppose I shouldn't have been surprised that afternoon when the doorbell rang. When I opened it, I found them standing on the doorstep. "Hey, Lily, how's your great-aunt?" Ariadne asked, but she was already pushing past me.

Before I could stop any of them, they had shoved past me and up the stairs.

I raced up after them. "Hey, come back here," I said. "She's busy."

"We'll wait," Akeem said, looking around for Auntie. He and Barry must have come up from their kung fu lessons, because they were dressed in black pants and white T-shirts.

At the bottom of the stairs, the door slammed loudly, and I saw Linda. "The door slipped out of my hand," she said apologetically.

I swung around on Ariadne. "She's not even on our team."

"She tagged along." Ariadne shrugged, turning this way and that looking for a glimpse of my great-aunt.

Suddenly, from the living room, Auntie shouted, "What do you mean you can't have the costumes ready by the parade? I told you we need them now. Oh, yeah, well, you too." And she slammed the phone down loudly.

My classmates exchanged looks with me. "Maybe we'd better go," Ariadne whispered.

At that moment, though, Auntie burst from the living room waving a sheaf of papers over her head and leaving a trail of scraps and Post-its behind her on the hallway floor. "Who let in the herd of buffalo?" she demanded angrily. "How can a person think?"

I tried to head off trouble by apologizing. "I'm sorry, Auntie. These are some of my classmates, but they were just leaving."

Though it was afternoon, Auntie was wearing silk pajamas under her satin robe, and her usual makeup. When she saw she had an audience, she posed almost regally. "You must pardon me. I've had a little setback." She tapped me with the papers. "Lily, won't you introduce me?"

As I did, my classmates kept silent, staring at Auntie as if she were a wax statue in some museum. When I was finished, she flashed her most dazzling smile. "Charmed."

"Can . . . can I have your autograph?" Linda asked, holding up a sheet of paper.

I was going to scold her for being a pest, but Akeem eagerly thrust another sheet at Auntie. "Me too," he said.

Auntie seemed pleased as she set down her papers on the floor. "I'd be happy to."

For a moment, she was surrounded by sheets of paper, fluttering from hands like large pale moths.

"How did you get your nickname, anyway?" Ariadne asked.

"Our school decided to do a production of *Peter Pan*," Auntie said as she kept on signing. "Naturally I tried out for Wendy, which is the female lead, but with this skin they decided to make me Tiger Lily."

"That isn't right." Ariadne bristled.

"No, and I've been apologizing to my Native American friends since," Auntie said. "But I did get a nickname out of it."

When she was finished, she clasped her hands in front of her. "You have to excuse me if I'm a bit grouchy. Every time the weather changes, I get headaches. I've gotten them ever since I was in Africa."

"When were you there?" Ariadne asked.

Auntie looked over their heads toward the street as if she could see Africa just outside our window. "Years ago, when I was making a movie."

Akeem squirmed a little closer. "What was it?"

"Some Tarzan flick." Auntie struck a pose. "I was a mermaid." And then she laughed. "A spear carrier. Third one from the right."

Akeem frowned, pulling a printout from his back pocket. "That's not on the list."

"Of my movies?" Auntie asked, flattered, and held out her hand. When Akeem had given it to her, she scanned it quickly. "There's lots that got left off, kiddo."

They ended up staying two hours, listening as Auntie told one funny story after another.

As my classmates sat enthralled, I realized that Auntie wasn't the snob—I was. At least she had the manners to be civil to my classmates, and I could have hugged her for that.

# CHAPTER FIVE

All of us were surprised when Mom got home. "I didn't realize it was that late," Linda said, jumping to her feet.

Ariadne apologized to Auntie. "We kept you so busy talking that we kept you from getting your costumes done."

Auntie studied the top sheet of the papers. It was the Lion Salve costumes. "Now where can I get a dozen costumes sewn?"

As Akeem and Barry headed for the stairs, Ariadne dug her elbow into my side. "I wish I had a relative like her. She's great."

"Thanks," I said. It was strange to have Ariadne envying me.

Ariadne paused at the head of the stairs. "Coming, Linda?"

Linda was hovering shyly next to Auntie. "I'll be along in a minute."

I found myself wondering what she was going to try and mooch now. Ariadne must have come to the same conclusion, because she gave me a sympathetic look before she began to skip down the steps. "'Bye then."

When she heard the front door slam, Linda cleared her throat. "My mother might be able to do the costumes."

So Linda really was a mooch. I had to resist the urge to grab her by the collar and toss her out.

Auntie asked eagerly, "She can sew?"

"Like magic." Linda began to go through Auntie's designs and specs for costumes. The next moment she held up a sheet that seemed to show the understructure for the costume. "But my mother couldn't build this."

Auntie flapped a hand in dismissal. "The costumer's already done that. We just need the outer skins sewn together."

"Has the cloth been purchased?" Linda asked, sounding very professional.

"Yes," Auntie said.

Linda studied the sketch critically. "Have the pieces been cut?"

"No," Auntie admitted. "Will that be a problem?"

Linda set down the sketch with a sigh. "Before the costumes can be assembled, the pieces have to be marked on the cloth and cut. That's a little bit like designing a jigsaw puzzle, because you want to get the most pieces from one piece of cloth. Marking and cutting will take more time. But we can do all that."

Though I didn't like Linda much, I was willing to pitch in for Auntie's sake. "I could help," I volunteered.

"No," Linda said sharply—almost as if she were afraid.

"What's the big deal?" I wondered, puzzled by Linda's reaction. "I know how to cut along a line. I'll come to your house."

Linda acted as if I had just proposed robbing a bank. "That's impossible."

I thought again of what Ariadne had said—that no one had ever been a guest in Linda's home—and I wondered what the problem was.

Determined to change the subject, Linda turned to Auntie. "When will you have the cloth?"

"We can have it tomorrow," Auntie said. "I'll have Lily's mom close up her shop and drive me. Where would you like me to drop it off?"

"No, no, I'd rather pick it up myself," Linda said, still keeping her home life a mystery.

Auntie studied Linda shrewdly. "It's just us three girls from Chinatown now. What are you worried about?" She made it sound as if we three belonged to an exclusive club.

I wanted to object. Linda might be from Chinatown, but I had always lived above it. I had more in common with Ariadne than I did with Linda. And Auntie had been away from Chinatown longer than I had lived.

It's not like I was prejudiced against J.O.J.s. It was just that they were . . . well . . . different. All the foreign-born Chinese kids were. Sometimes they seemed like a separate species.

Linda glanced at me as if she didn't count me as one of her kind either, and then she took in Auntie's clothes, makeup and hairdo. "What do you know about Chinatown?"

"I know that it wouldn't be any problem to stop by the projects," Auntie said smoothly.

Linda gave a start. "How did you know where I lived?"

Auntie lifted a shoulder and dropped it again. "Because when I was your age, kiddo, I acted the same way—only the tenement we lived in wasn't half as nice as a project. There was only one toilet to a floor, for one thing."

Though I knew our families had had it rough, neither Mom nor Dad would talk about those days. And now it was hard to believe my glamorous great-aunt had worn anything but silk and satin. "Really?" I asked.

Auntie winked at me. "Just don't tell your mom that I told you, okay, kiddo? I don't think she wants people to know about that part of our family's past."

"When you were young, were all the other girls at school rich?" Linda asked her.

"Compared to us they were," Auntie said with an encouraging smile. "I used to be so afraid they'd make fun of me."

"Yes," Linda agreed eagerly. "They just wouldn't understand."

"Some of them might," I said softly. "If you ever spoke to them."

Linda colored as she glanced over her shoulder at me uncertainly. "I've already said too much."

Auntie caught her hand as she started to get up and made her sit down again. "All right. Suit yourself. Let's get back to business. I'm sorry that I have to ask this, but I don't have time for another failure: What are your mother's qualifications?"

"She . . . she sews very well," Linda insisted.

"Yes, you said like magic." Auntie leaned forward. "But this job is more than sewing a dress for you from some pattern. I have to be sure she can do it by the parade, or I'll have to find someone professional."

"But she is a professional," Linda protested.

Auntie arched an eyebrow. "A costumer?"

"No, she works . . ." Linda hesitated as she looked unhappily at me again. "She works at the Happy Fortune."

She stared at Auntie as if she were hoping the name was familiar to Auntie, but Auntie shook her head. "I've been away from Chinatown for a long time. I don't think I know that place."

"It's a _____," Linda confessed in a small voice. She used a Chinese phrase I didn't recognize and couldn't pronounce.

"What's that?" I asked Auntie, puzzled.

Auntie knew the term. "In English it's called a sweatshop. Sweatshops are mini factories where clothes are sewn together. Some of the fanciest American designer

43

labels have their clothes assembled there. But the women who sew the garments get paid by the piece."

Even though I had to ask, I didn't think I was going to like the answer. "What's that?"

"They get paid by the garment rather than by the hour," Auntie said. "So a woman has to sew very fast to scrape by."

I glanced at Linda guiltily. No wonder Linda never had money for movies and always brought her own lunch. I felt bad for thinking she was a mooch. "Ariadne's grandmother worked in the garment district in New York," I said.

Linda seemed to gather courage from that. "Really?"

"You should talk with her sometime," I suggested. "I bet her stories would be a lot like your mom's."

"It's rough for anybody when they've just come here." Linda seemed to be encouraged when Auntie nodded her head. "Please—my family needs the work."

"Is she going to be laid off?" Auntie asked sympathetically.

Linda's head dipped in embarrassment. "No, but she and her friends haven't been paid in three months."

"Three months?" I said in amazement. "Is that legal?" I felt even more ashamed for judging her so harshly.

Linda shrugged philosophically. "The foreman says the owners have had unexpected expenses."

"I think we need to get them a good lawyer, kiddo," Auntie said. "I know some good ones who will work *pro bono*."

"*Pro bono?*" Linda asked.

"For the public good," Auntie explained. "That means they'll do it for free."

"My mother wouldn't want to . . ." Linda paused as she hunted for the right idiom. "To rock the boat."

"Well"—Auntie sat back with a sigh—"when she's ready to shake things up, you let me know. In the meantime, she can do the costumes. Pick up the material tomorrow. I'll pay you what I was going to pay the costumer." She mentioned a figure.

Linda brightened when she heard the price. "We won't let you down," she promised. "Even if we have to sew all night at home."

"See you tomorrow," I said as she was going out.

She walked down two steps and then stopped and swung around. We were about eye level at that point. "Please don't mention the sewing to anyone," she said.

"Not even Ariadne?" I asked.

"Especially Ariadne," Linda said.

I watched her descend the stairs heavily and shut the door. I was still standing there when Auntie joined me. "Here's your coat, kiddo," she said, thrusting it into my hands.

I turned to see Auntie already had hers on. "Where are we going?"

"Just for a short walk. I want to explain why you have to respect Linda's wishes and keep quiet," she said as she helped me into my coat.

The night air was crisp and cold. Before us, the

street plunged straight down into Chinatown like black velvet stretched taut over the rolling, dipping side of the hill. It reminded me of the panther at the zoo, whose black, velvety fur covered but did not hide the muscles. And the streetlamps and the lights in the office buildings looked like golden beads. Even the garish neon signs glowed like fragments of rainbows.

And now that they had torn down the old Embarcadero freeway, we could look across the bay, where the lights of Oakland burned like piles of gold dust. Even the Bay Bridge looked pretty in the evening, outfitted with lights that spanned it like a shining necklace.

Auntie pointed out the roofs of the projects. "Your parents are so proud that they made their way up the hill. But don't ever forget where your family came from."

All around us were houses that belonged to my parents' classmates. I knew them well enough to call them uncles and aunts in a kind of extended family. I knew that they had all gone to school together from kindergarten all the way through high school—and just like my parents, they had lived in the low-cost housing projects or even worse places like Auntie and had worked their way "up the hill" too. They were the third- and fourth-generation descendants of the Chinese who had first come to San Francisco, but they had bought houses on the slopes of Nob Hill, where they could gaze down on the Chinatown projects they had left.

Suddenly I began to understand a little bit of my

parents' pride. "Mom and Dad did pretty good, didn't they?" I whispered to Auntie.

"Better than you know," Auntie said, pointing to a cable car as it lurched along Powell Street. "There was a time when no one would rent to a Chinese above here. No matter how rich you were."

"So Linda has nothing to be ashamed of," I said.

"I was like Linda at one time." Auntie said. "I look at your mom or Linda, and I see a path that I didn't take." She nodded down at the arched roofs. "But you know what? All those paths start right down there."

In a way, now, I took it as a compliment that Auntie had called me a Chinatown girl—even if I wasn't. And suddenly it made me feel sad that it wasn't true. Like I was empty while Linda was full.

"Maybe she'll get over it someday," Auntie said. "Most of us do. Without hope, you're nothing, kiddo. In the meantime, let her play it her way."

Cheeks tingling, we turned back to our house, where the warmth and the good smells of Mom's cooking rolled down the steps like a glove to draw us in.

# CHAPTER SIX

T he next day Linda was silent and withdrawn at school, avoiding me as much as she could. And when she came by to pick up the material after school, she hardly spoke to either me or Auntie. It was as if she were ashamed of having confessed too much. I wanted to tell her there was nothing to be embarrassed about—that Auntie had explained and I understood. And yet what did I really understand?

What if my parents had not been successful? I might be Linda's neighbor. What did I really know about Chinatown except where to shop for food and candy? Like a lot of other kids, I assumed it was a place where immigrants and poor losers lived.

I found myself becoming more and more curious about the way Linda lived. Sometimes I even thought of Linda as living the life I might have lived: Chinatown girl.

In the meantime, the parade had become a political

football while the supervisors debated the matter. Supervisor Macek was all over the tube calling for a ban on the parade. Coached by Auntie, Mrs. Wong got almost as much airtime. Making a point of wearing the Goblin Pearls, she made herself into a representative of all the law-abiding Chinese.

The Powell Street Boys didn't give interviews. Instead, they robbed a bank—taking the display of ancient priceless coins from the bank's window. Everyone figured they were developing a taste for antiques—a taste that might include the Goblin Pearls.

Backed by the fearless Mrs. Wong, Auntie led the fight to save the parade. The climax was when she gave an impassioned plea to the supervisors. "If you vote to ban the parade," she told them, "you will let down every citizen who trusts in the system to protect us. Not just Chinese Americans, but all Americans, because the parade draws people of all colors and faiths. You will be turning your backs upon Americans"—and she made a point of waving a hand at Mrs. Wong—"who follow the laws. You will be letting a band of hooligans dictate our lives."

In the end, Supervisor Macek withdrew his proposal.

"You see," Dad said to Chris, "we're not doormats. We get what we want nowadays."

Chris had only smiled sourly. "Supervisor Macek got as much mileage as he could out of the cancellation. He made points with the law-and-order folks and got a lot of free time on camera, so everyone will recognize him."

Despite Chris' pessimism, our New Year's banquet that year also had the air of a victory celebration. (My family wasn't particularly religious, so New Year's boiled down to a big family get-together—at which Auntie entertained.)

And then came the fateful Saturday afternoon of the parade. The morning had begun when Linda rang the doorbell. We stared at one another when I opened the door. There was a lot I wanted to ask her, and I think there was a lot she wanted to tell, but neither of us was brave enough to take the first step.

She only nodded to several shopping bags at her feet. "I brought the costumes."

I looked at them. They looked like giant inkblots. "Great. Let me give you a hand."

Auntie had been prowling the floor waiting for Linda. She pounced on one of the bags as soon as we had brought them up. "Good, very good," she said as she spread it out.

After Auntie had written out the check, Linda clutched it. "Thank you. We're ever so grateful to you."

Auntie patted her cheek. "I'm the one who's grateful. Has your mother been paid her back wages?"

Linda tucked the check away in her wallet carefully. "Not yet."

"Maybe you do need a lawyer," Auntie said. "I can suggest a few."

"I told her about your offer. My mother quoted an

old proverb: 'Better to hold a tiger by the tail than go to court,'" Linda said. "She's a little old-fashioned."

"Well, if you ever change your mind, I'll give you some names," Auntie offered again.

A little after Linda left, the firecrackers began going off in Chinatown. It sounded like a regular battlefield against goblins in the streets below us. Were the Powell Street Boys hiding out there someplace?

Through the window I could see dark clouds rolling across the sky as if there were going to be another battle up there.

"It looks like rain, Auntie," I said, turning away from the living-room window.

Auntie was busy pulling one of the costumes over the understructure. "Well, the parade has a dragon, and dragons bring storms."

"You've gone to a lot of trouble for Mr. Soo," I said. "He must be a good friend."

"Actually, I've only met him a couple of times." Auntie tugged at a seam, testing it. "But the man is beaucoup bucks, so maybe sometime he'd like to throw some away by investing in a movie. The biggest challenge of making a movie is raising the money for it."

"What movie would you like to do?" I asked curiously.

Auntie hesitated and then almost shyly confessed, "The best lines in my movies were ad libs, kiddo. So eventually I wrote my own script for Tiger Lil, but I could never get the studio interested in it."

"But you are Tiger Lil," I protested.

"Yes, and I'd like to do her my way. But the studio preferred to play it safe by following the formula. The plots for my movies were all pretty interchangeable with the other films back then—Charlie Chan, Mr. Moto, Mr. Wong." She ticked them off on her fingers. "Except that the others had whites playing the lead roles."

I remembered what Chris had first said about the limitations of Auntie's roles. It was the first hint I had that maybe Chris had been right, and the rest of us had been wrong. "So what would you have done differently?" I asked.

"Set it in the real Chinatown—not someplace created by a hack writer." Auntie waved her hand toward Chinatown down the hill. "James Wong Howe himself said I had the leverage."

Talking to Auntie sometimes made me feel as if I were learning a foreign language—all of those names from the past. "Who?"

Auntie sighed sadly. "You kids have really forgotten him, haven't you? He set an example for all of us. Mr. Howe could do anything with a camera, and he won two Oscars for it. Barbra Streisand herself coaxed him out of retirement just to shoot her in *Hello, Dolly*."

For once we had something in common. "I've seen that on television," I said.

"But I waited too long," Auntie said softly. "And then it was too late."

"What do you mean?" I asked.

"You don't want to hear about ancient history, kiddo." I think Auntie felt she had already revealed too much, because she turned away brusquely, setting down one costume and picking up the next.

At that moment, though, a neighbor began setting off firecrackers next door.

Because of the explosions, I didn't hear the phone ringing at first, but Auntie did. "Will you get the phone, kiddo?"

When I answered it, I had to put a hand over my exposed ear to hear the caller. If I had known the effect the conversation would have on our lives, I would have bolted for the door.

As it was, I returned in all innocence to the living room after hanging up. "Sally can't make it, Auntie."

Auntie put down the costume. "What do you mean she can't make it? She has to. She'll throw off the formation."

I picked my way between the two rows of costume jars laid out like soldiers. "She hurt her ankle skating in the park this morning. She says she's sorry."

Auntie scrutinized the costumes and then swung her gaze toward me with a strange, obsessed gleam in her eye. "Hmm, Sally was a petite. You're about the same size as her."

I wanted to please Auntie, but I knew I would fail. And what about the Powell Street Boys? Their target, the Goblin Pearls, would be right in the middle of Auntie's float. "I'm not an actor, Auntie."

Auntie set her hands on my shoulders. "Nonsense. I see 'jarness' positively fighting to get out from inside you."

I didn't want to be in the middle of a battlefield. Desperately I began to babble, "But I think it's going to rain tonight, and I think I have the beginnings of a cold."

Auntie nodded to her large, klutzy bag leaning against one wall. "I've got disposable booties for all the actors, and the jar will protect you from the rain."

No matter how I tried to worm out of it, there was just no way of refusing my famous great-aunt when she had her mind set on something. That single-mindedness, as Mom had often told me, had made her a legend.

Even as I kept protesting, the legend herself pulled my sweater over my head. "There are some who are born to greatness, and there are some who have greatness thrust upon them. Well, tag, you're it."

I jumped when I heard dozens of firecrackers. Someone was setting off a whole string. Suddenly there was the siren of a police car. The cops weren't going to tolerate firecrackers this early in the day. The goblins were safe for now.

# CHAPTER SEVEN

Even though the parade route and Chinatown were crawling with cops, I tried one last time to get out of it at the assembly area. "This is shanghaiing, in case you didn't know," I informed Auntie Tiger Lil. "And it's illegal in most countries."

"You don't hear the other actors complaining," she coaxed in Chinese. "They're all professionals."

A dozen walking jars of Lion Salve milled about in the street. Some were blue-labeled jars and others were white. The only parts you could see of us were our legs clad in black tights and black cloth kung fu shoes.

Inside the giant cylinder, as I fussed with the straps of my costume, I decided it was hard to have a famous relative. I had found it impossible to turn her down when she asked me to do her a favor. Since my own Chinese was pretty bad, I replied in English. "I don't know if I would call this acting," I said doubtfully.

Eyeholes had been strategically punched into the

cylinder where the lion dog on the label would have its eyes. Unfortunately, I had to lean over to look out, and whenever I leaned over, the whole costume tilted. If I went past a certain point, the jar had its own momentum and I fell. I had already fallen twice, but both times Auntie Tiger Lil had managed to repair the dents.

"How many times do I have to tell you?" Auntie Tiger Lil tried to encourage me. "There are no small parts, only small actors."

I understood more Chinese than I could speak. "And how many times do I have to tell you? I'm no actor." I was so exasperated that I wound up hopping up and down. Big mistake. The costume kept moving even after I had stopped.

Auntie put her hands on the top and stilled my costume. "We all start out in bit parts, kiddo. This is opportunity knocking." When she rapped her knuckles against the jar's side, I felt like I was in a drum.

Mom stepped off a curb and into the street. "Lily, is that you?"

"She'll be safe," Auntie promised her. "I'll be right with her."

Through one of the slits, I saw Mom's face. Fear warred with hero worship.

"Mrs. Wong trusts Auntie enough to put her own daughter at the center of the target," Dad pointed out. In the end, Mom's faith in Auntie won out.

"I suppose we ought to get a record of this," Mom said as she got out her camera.

"No, Mom." For emphasis, I wagged the jar from side to side.

Auntie Tiger Lil wrapped her left arm around the jar so I could not move. "Be a sport."

Mom crouched and aimed the camera. "Smile. I mean you, Auntie, not Lily."

"Cheese," Auntie Tiger Lil said.

With a sigh, I decided to make the best of it. After all, it wasn't like I was getting up on the float with the pearls around my neck. I was just one of a dozen jars of Lion Salve. "And crackers," I said—though a fat lot of good it did to smile. I saw the flash of the camera even in here.

Before Auntie let go, she promised, "I'll make it up to you, kiddo."

Just a few encouraging words from my famous great-aunt and I instantly felt better. "It okay," I mumbled in my broken Chinese.

"Now you have your picture taken with your sister," Dad said to Chris.

"I wouldn't be caught dead with her."

Mom spoke up before he could start an argument with Dad. "It's New Year's, Chris," she wheedled. "Let's not have a fight."

"That's just it," Chris said, folding his arms. "New Year's is almost over. This parade is just for tourists. It makes the rest of America think that's all we are— quaint curiosities." He pointed at a band of uniformed musicians climbing off huge, air-conditioned buses. On the sides were painted signs proclaiming them to be a prize-winning band from across the bay over in the white suburbs. "Look. They're not even Chinese."

"Now listen here, young man." Dad began to wag his finger at Chris.

Mom stopped him. "He's just at the tail end of the difficult years."

"You hope," Dad growled, but he subsided.

In the distance we heard the pop of a firecracker. "Remember the old days?" Mom asked, trying to distract him. "People used to set off thousands of firecrackers."

"You'd be ankle deep in bits of red paper," Dad agreed. From far away came the sound of a police siren. "But not anymore. The police get you."

"Still, the parade never used to be this fancy," Mom said.

"Isn't there a photo of Dad as a boy in a white shirt and gray slacks?" Chris wondered. "He was marching with a group of children who each had a balloon. And on every balloon was written Happy New Year."

"He was so cute then," Mom said, and nudged Dad. "I guess parades are a tradition in this family."

At least I would have an incriminating photo of one other member of our family. Reassured, I started to look around. Up to now, I had always watched the parade on television, because the thought of the huge crowds made me feel queasy.

I felt as if I were deep inside a canyon formed by tall buildings rising on either side that shut out all but a narrow strip of the night sky. There were small stores and cafes at ground level and offices above; but it wasn't the best part of downtown. The typewriters in the window of the repair shop were gathering dust. And the cafes were the kind that made most of their money selling lottery tickets and handled stale sandwiches and canned soda as an afterthought—though for the occasion, they had covered up all the prices on their signboards and jacked up everything by a buck.

In the street, the parade was assembling, so there was a constant jangling of timpani and glockenspiels. Boys and girls from the various martial arts studios were practicing kicks and shouts till their faces turned red. Others were playing with their swords and spears—I just hoped they were stage weapons and didn't have any real sharp points or edges.

Stilt walkers in long robes practiced a few steps without their papier-mâché heads. There were the Eight Immortals and various heroes. And since this was the Year of the Pig, a character called Pigsy was very popular. He was one of the friends of the Monkey King. His head was typically a papier-mâché mask, which bobbed like those old toy dolls that people used to have in the back windows of their cars.

Pigsy was kept busy waving at sweatshirted kids in little pig snouts and ears. Teachers were marshaling them together in parade units. And everywhere people in masks and costumes flitted about. At home, seen on a television screen, they would have looked like people in fancy getups. But seen up close and in the darkening light, the garish colors of their masks and costumes seemed natural, and they seemed to tower over me like the stilt walkers. I would have sworn that there were all sorts of ghosts and spirits and goblins unsettled by the New Year.

Here and there, some nervous drummer tried a quick tattoo like a string of firecrackers going off to drive away the spirits and goblins. From somewhere else the big lion dance drums boomed in answer like rolling thunder. Or was that from overhead? I looked up nervously at the sky. The clouds were almost black, ready to rain at any moment. If ever there was an evening for goblins, this was it.

The girls from St. Mary's drum corps were a bit behind us. St. Mary's was my mother's old school, and she had been in the drum corps there. They wore bright costumes of red and yellow with headdresses of colored pom-poms. Though I went to a public school, I had a few friends from the neighborhood who were in the drum corps. I used to razz them regularly about putting on their outfits. I just hoped they didn't realize it was me inside this jar, or I'd never hear the end of it.

Contrary to what Chris had said, there were a lot of Chinese in the parade. Some of them I knew because they lived in Chinatown. Others were schoolmates who lived in other areas of the city but had come in for the parade. And there were some I'd never seen before— kids whose Chinese was even worse than mine or didn't speak it at all. I figured they were what Chris called sub-urban Chinese, who lived away from the city in big sub-divisions of ranch houses. The only time they usually showed their faces in Chinatown was to visit older relatives who still lived here. But somehow, they had gotten drafted into the parade just as I had.

San Francisco, though, was a city that loved parties, so there were other groups celebrating Chinese New Year. There was a group of marching hula dancers and a group of samba dancers in skimpy costumes—Chris stopped complaining about "outsiders" after he saw them. A band of accordion players was practicing the chords of "Lady of Spain."

There were also long lines before the row of Porta Potties. Suddenly I began to wonder how to free myself from the costume. "Auntie," I called frantically.

"What is it, kiddo?" Auntie asked as she bustled over.

Seeing my frantic bobbing, Dad joined us with Mom. "You okay, honey?"

As bad luck would have it, Auntie's client picked that moment to arrive. Mr. Soo was a small man in an impeccably tailored blue suit. Auntie had said his herbal remedy could cure more aches and pains and ills than its rival, Tiger Balm.

"Wonderful, Miss Leung. Absolutely wonderful," he called in an elegant English accent. He paused on the curb for the star of our float, Clark Tom, who still had a wine glass in his hand. Auntie had pulled out all the stops for Mr. Soo by bringing the most popular Chinese American actor into the project.

When Mom saw him, all thought of my welfare flew out of her head. "Come on, Henry." Hooking her arm through Dad's, she dragged him over there.

I couldn't help feeling a little twinge when I saw him, and so did most of the girls in the drum corps, who began turning and pointing excitedly. He was very handsome and should have been more than the sidekick in *East Meets West*. His trademark remark, "Gotcha," had become a national catchword.

"Sorry, kiddo," Auntie muttered. "Duty calls." And she hurried off to welcome her client and her celebrity.

"I just hope nature doesn't call," I muttered.

"What's holding things up? I'm already covered in sweat," a man said in English to me.

I turned slowly to see that it was another jar of Lion Salve.

Someone tapped on the side of my costume. "Eyes front," Auntie Tiger Lil chided me in English. She had come back.

I shifted my feet so I could face forward in time to see Auntie Tiger Lil with Linda.

"I just came by to see how the costumes were," Linda said.

"Marvelous," Auntie said. "Your mother did excellent work. But where is she?"

"She had to work on a rush order," Linda said.

"During the New Year's parade?" Auntie clicked

62

her tongue. "The owners must be related to Scrooge."

"Well, really, New Year's is just about over," Linda observed. "So I told my mother I'd describe it to her."

I tried to be as inconspicuous as I could inside a giant jar of Lion Salve, afraid Auntie would call me over to meet Linda.

Next to me, the man said, "You don't sound like Sally."

"I'm an emergency replacement," I said hurriedly in a low voice, afraid that Linda would overhear. "Lucky Sally got sick."

"A gig's a gig," he said.

"You're not scared of the Powell Street Boys?" I asked.

"A good professional doesn't worry about stuff like that. I've been in a St. Patrick's, a Columbus Day, and a Carnival parade." He rattled off a half dozen product names. "But," he added proudly, "I really got noticed for my car wax."

I didn't know what to say except "Congratulations."

"Besides," he added, "they've got cops every ten feet along the parade route. And there's a SWAT team in reserve. This is probably the safest place in town."

I tried to take his reassurances to heart. "I guess."

"Incidentally, my name's Norm," the man said.

"Mine's Lily Lew."

When I looked back, I saw Auntie had bustled off on some new errand while Linda was wandering through the crowds toward Clark. Some of the girls from the drum corps had put down their instruments and gone over to get Clark's autograph on envelopes or napkins or whatever they could improvise.

"Get away from me, you little rats." He waved his free hand so violently that he wobbled and would have fallen without Mr. Soo's help.

"He's drunk," I gasped to Norm.

"You see that sometimes at the trade shows. You get some kid that's put in the spotlight for his good looks, and all the while he hates it." Norm bumped against me. "Just remember, Lily. There are no small parts—"

"—only small actors," I finished. "Yeah, I know."

"The trick," Norm explained, "is to be the best Lion Salve you can be. I'm playing it proud and yet helpful. Kind of Alan Alda. What about you?"

"Norm, guess what." I didn't wait for him to answer. "I hate the stuff. I have an uncle who swears by it for his rheumatism, but you wouldn't want him to get upwind of you."

"It doesn't matter," Norm insisted. "We're selling a dream."

I wondered what Auntie would have done in my place. She would have agreed with Norm: Be the best jar you could be. That was how she had risen to be a top Hollywood star.

I did a little stutter step and turned enough to glance at Norm. He was standing proudly, full of vim and vigor, and yet his jar was inclined forward slightly as if he were ready to ooze salve over the nearest injured person.

I decided to make Auntie glad she had picked me. At twelve, I knew I was too short to be proud and dignified. It was better to be cute.

As I was planning my routine, Miss Lion Salve finally reached us. Her name was Tiffany Wong.

Through one of the view slits of my costume, I saw Chris go all goofy—he actually had a pleasant smile for a change when he said hello to someone. "Hello, Tiffany."

"Oh . . . hello . . . um . . ." Tiffany said. She had the same crisp, posh accent as her mother. She studied him as if she could not quite place him.

Tiffany was a year ahead of him in high school, and I think he had a crush on her. So did most of the boys in Chinatown, because she was a knockout and had even done some modeling for the local department stores. As Miss Lion Salve, she got to ride on the float.

"Wait a moment, darling," Mrs. Wong said. "The Goblin Pearls are crooked. Wear our pearls with pride tonight." She made a great show of rearranging the string of pearls that encircled Tiffany's neck.

Tiffany fussed with her gown. "Technically they're not our pearls. They belong to Happy Fortune Enterprises."

I tried to think of where I had heard that name, Happy Fortune, before; and then I remembered Linda's mother. So the Wongs were the owners of the sweatshop—though from what Dad had said earlier, it sounded as if they had branched out from making clothes into real estate. As I stared at the pearls, I wondered if they were part of the "unexpected expenses" that had kept the Wongs from paying their workers.

I studied Tiffany with new interest, wondering just how many others the Wongs had cheated in order to pay for her fancy clothes. Or maybe she had had her mother run up an extra designer costume for her. And how would she react if I told her the Goblin Pearls were probably bought with money that should have gone to a lot of poor women like Linda's mother?

"To the crown jewel of all their possessions." Clark started to lift his glass in a toast to Tiffany, but he didn't have enough control. Instead of raising the glass slightly, his arm shot up, splashing wine all over the front of her dress.

"My gown," Tiffany gasped.

"My pearls," her mother shouted.

"It's no problem. No problem," Auntie tried to insist.

She set her big black leather bag down on the sidewalk. It was bulging with plastic bottles of water, bandages and Lion Salve for her ailing troops. I knew what was in it because I had helped pack it.

Ripping open a bandage, she handed Dad a bottle of water. "Open that, Henry." When he did, she wet the bandage and began daubing at Tiffany's clothes and jewelry.

In the meantime, Tiffany was growing hysterical. "Everything's ruined," she kept repeating as she held her arms from her sides.

At the same time, Mr. Soo kept saying as he patted her hand, "You just send the dry cleaning bill to me."

As people started to gather around them, Mrs. Wong snatched the bandage from Auntie. "Give that to me," she said savagely. She mopped at Tiffany's dress.

As she began working, a man in a blue robe pushed his way through the crowd. His face was completely covered by a green goblin mask with a hideous leer. The Powell Street Boys had called the city's bluff.

Shoving Mrs. Wong out of the way, the Powell Street Boy seized the pearls around Tiffany's neck. With a yank, he pulled them away from her just as Mrs. Wong fell on her fundamentals.

"Help! Thief!" Mrs. Wong shouted.

Auntie Tiger Lil's face got an expression I had seen in a film just before she ordered somebody's head chopped off. Despite the heat inside the costume, I felt a little shiver pass up my spine. In the short time she'd been staying with us, I'd quickly learned that Auntie Tiger Lil was the one person you never crossed.

Norm knew it too. "Uh-huh," he grunted.

Though Auntie was small, she had a voice that could carry across one of those large Hong Kong–style restaurants that are built like auditoriums. And of course at MGM, she'd had voice and diction coaches, so her enunciation was impeccable and cut clear across the parade noise. "Come back here," Auntie shouted as she chased the thief.

"Auntie Tiger Lil. You don't have your stunt double here," I yelled as I started after her.

# CHAPTER EIGHT

"Stop, thief!" Auntie shouted as she pounded after the masked man. Behind our float was a contingent from a kung fu school. About half of the boys and girls were Chinese, but the others were Hispanic or white or Afro-American. They all just stood there and gaped as the Powell Street Boy ran by, followed by Auntie. Their jaws dropped even lower as I chugged along behind in my jar costume.

The next group was a bunch of six-year-olds in pig noses and ears. The children squealed as I staggered among them. I saw a blond woman holding several of them to her sides. "Sorry," I called to her.

Releasing the children, she stepped right in front of me angrily. She had a nose and ears to match the kids'. "Is this some kind of publicity stunt?"

Some people on the sidewalk overheard and began to laugh and applaud.

"No, it's not," I swore. "Please let me by. My auntie's in danger."

Over her shoulder, I could see the head of the Powell Street Boy bobbing as he plowed through a band. And behind the Powell Street Boy plodded Auntie, still bellowing for him to stop. To my frustration, the distance between us was growing.

"You just witnessed a real crime, madam," I said. "This isn't a reenactment."

"Really?" the woman said, hesitating. Her ears quivered.

As the distance increased between me and Auntie, I figured this was no time for manners. "Yes, ma'am. And I'm sorry, but this is an emergency. Coming through." Lowering my jar, I lurched forward. I felt the costume connect with something solid and heard the woman shout, followed by a thump.

I was afraid I'd wind up the same way as the woman, but I managed to regain my balance and straighten up. Majorettes in silver mesh swim suits were trying to even out their line. "Pardon me. Coming through," I shouted as I aimed for a gap.

The majorettes were more nimble than the woman and skipped out of the way like a school of fish. Suddenly a surprised drum major loomed before me with his large staff.

"Watch out," he warned the band. "There's a jar on the loose now."

The band had just begun straightening their ranks.

Flutes and fifes got out of the way easily, but the tubas and bass drums had a harder time—even with advance warning.

For a moment I felt as if I were standing still in a forest of trees that were falling and crashing all around me in a huge storm. Drums boomed like thunder and brass instruments flashed like lightning bolts. And then I stumbled free into an open space.

Ahead of me was a combined group of lion dancers from several studios. The huge drums were on wheels so the assistants could push them along as the drummers played.

A half dozen lions had been practicing. These weren't like the lions in the zoo, but stylized, so one had a mane of bright scarlet hair while another had blue. Their face masks were painted in rainbow colors, and their big eyes bounced like huge white balls.

Each lion had a dancer and a partner to hold the cape that hung from the lion's head. More dancers stood on either side to relieve the main dancers. All of them were dressed in loose black pants and cloth shoes with white T-shirts.

They were standing around in confusion. "Excuse me, pardon me, coming through," I kept repeating over and over.

To my mortification, my classmate Barry was there as an assistant to one of the lions. "Hey," he objected as I rammed my way past him.

I was congratulating myself upon my narrow escape

71

when Linda darted from the sidewalk, trotting along beside me.

"Lily, is that you?" she asked.

Desperately I wagged the jar from side to side negatively.

However, she squatted down, peeking up under the costume. "It is you," she said triumphantly. "Don't lie."

"Leave me alone," I groaned as I stumbled on with the costume straps cutting into my shoulders. I'd have a lot to live down at school on Monday.

Ahead of me was a group of girls in pink silk slacks and blouses with sequin designs. With them was a woman in green with pink toe shoes. "She caught him," she said to the girls.

I didn't know if that was good news or not. And though my legs were getting tired and the costume was getting heavy, I tried to pick up speed.

Just ahead of me was the St. Mary's drum corps intermingled with another bunch of lion dancers—as if Auntie's cometlike passage had mixed the groups together like grains of sand. Among the girls were about twenty boys and men holding up what looked like a white telephone pole almost twenty feet high. Projecting from the sides of the pole were smaller sticks to act as rungs. Halfway up the pole, a courageous boy stood on the rungs, holding up the lion's head as he peered behind him with everyone else. His cape was held up by another boy who had a long bamboo pole. Another boy held a huge glittering ball on top of another pole.

The golden dragon brought up the "tail end" of the parade, as everyone liked to joke. The costume was over a hundred feet long, with a huge dragon's head and bobbing eyes. To be honest, it looked kind of gaudy in the twilight with all the light bulbs sticking out on the papier-mâché face and sides. Because it was so long, the costume snaked back and forth across the street so it wouldn't take up so much room; and it looked for the moment like a broken store sign.

The team that helped the dragon dancers was standing and pointing, while the dozens of boys and men in the costume crouched, trying to peer out from underneath it.

The Powell Street Boy had finally come up against something he could not dart straight through, and in trying to dodge to the side, he had let Auntie catch up to him.

They stood now, toe-to-toe, face-to-face, like Godzilla versus Mega-Godzilla. In a heroic tug-of-war, the Powell Street Boy had a hand on either end of the necklace, trying to pull it out of Auntie's grasp.

With all these martial arts students around, it seemed silly for Auntie to be struggling all on her own.

"Don't just stand there," I shouted to the lion dancers. "Do something. Help my auntie. That's Tiger Lil."

By the dragon was a boy in pale-blue robes and a black satin vest. His head was covered by a giant papier-mâché head. In his hands, he gripped a pole topped by a glittering ball.

"Who's Tiger Lil?" he shouted back.

"She's the hero," I puffed.

Fortunately, he took my word for it. "My grandmother swears by your salve," he said. Crouching, he set his pole and ball on the ground and removed his head. I saw then that he looked about sixteen.

Nodding to some of his teammates, he moved forward with a half dozen boys, all of them also in black slacks and shoes and white T-shirts.

I tried to shout encouragement. "Hold on, Auntie."

Unfortunately, I couldn't see where my feet were going. I should have gone around the pole, but instead I tried to save time by skipping over it. Only I hadn't allowed for the weight of the oversize costume.

I landed short, tripping over it. In a panic, I tried to spread my arms to balance myself, but of course they only shoved against the sides of the jar.

I was helpless as I watched the black asphalt rush up toward me. The other times I'd fallen, Auntie Tiger Lil had been there to catch me.

My feet slid along the pavement as I tried to get a grip. Unfortunately, the rubber soles of the cloth shoes kept slipping.

To my horror, I started to roll.

# CHAPTER NINE

"Oncoming!" I heard Norm shouted in warning. He must have followed me.

The world spun by as I rolled along, trapped within the costume. Through the eye slits, I saw patches of black asphalt whirl by, giving way to the startled faces of the crowd.

Glockenspiels clanged and chimed all around me as they crashed to the street. Suddenly I knew what the clapper in a church bell must feel like on Sunday morning.

"Stop that jar," Norm called from behind me. I felt awful at wrecking the parade, but I was helpless to stop myself.

"Sorry, sorry," I kept apologizing until I couldn't feel any more bumps. Between the rolling and smell of the oil patches on the street, I started to feel sick. I realized suddenly that that was yet another thing the costume should have allowed for.

Suddenly from up ahead, a loud cheer rose up. I wondered if the parade was starting, but then I heard Auntie shout triumphantly, "They've got you. You might as well let go of the necklace."

When you're moving at street level, you're definitely grateful that there aren't any horse units in this parade. As I trundled along, I wondered if I would roll right into the bay. I could only hope the costume would float.

Just as I had begun to despair, the costume jerked to an abrupt halt, and I heard Auntie give a shout. "What's going on?" I yelled. And then I heard some loud grunts.

"Don't let him get away," Auntie called. She sounded close to the ground, as if she had fallen.

Funny, but my nose picked up the faint smell of cigar smoke. I thought it was odd, since most of the people in the parade were kids.

Since I had no arms to grab, I could only use my legs. I lashed out with my feet and felt them connect with someone's legs. To my chagrin, I heard Clark Tom yelp and fall.

Maybe the excitement had sobered him up real fast; but since his show always found excuses to strip him down to his trunks, I knew he had a good, athletic build. He'd easily outdistanced Norm in his costume and caught up with me.

Chris had joined us as well. "You okay, Auntie?"

"Oh, thank Heaven," Auntie puffed. "Help your sister, Chris."

Unlike Auntie, Chris had plenty of wind to crack jokes. "Sure. Which end goes up?"

"Get me out of here," I said, kicking my legs.

"I would, but I don't have a can opener," Chris teased.

"Ha ha! Remind me to a throw a penny at you." I tried to sit up, but strapped inside the costume, I was like a turtle on her back.

Then I could smell Clark's wine. He must have soaked in it. "Up you go," he said as his strong hands lifted me upright. There were plenty of girls in Chinatown who would have dreamed of being rescued by Clark—but not quite in this undignified way.

Once I was on my feet, I almost jumped when I saw a huge eyeball staring at me. Then I realized that I had been stopped by the dragon head itself. As anxious dragon dancers were inspecting it for damage, I tried to move a few steps away out of their sight.

In my mind, I had time to replay a little of the scene. It wasn't everyone who could wreck the New Year's parade and make a shambles of her auntie's publicity plans. I had wanted to make Auntie so proud of me, and instead I'd done the opposite.

"Just whose side are you on?" Chris said to me. "I had him until you tripped me. Now he got away."

I rotated slowly like a tank turret, looking for Auntie, and several dancers cringed and dodged away from me, unsure of what to expect. I felt mortified as I struggled to get out of the costume's straps. Once you're in a jar of Lion Salve, though, you're in it for good.

Finally, I saw her with her hair all tangled and her clothes all askew. "I'm so sorry. I let you down bad."

Auntie wrapped her arms around me desperately. "You didn't mess up. That thief got away, but we've got every television camera on us."

"What? Where?" Mortified, I twisted my head, trying to see through one of the eye slits.

"Smile and wave, Clark," Auntie ordered. "You're a hero."

Clark sounded bemused by my aunt. "Anytime."

Never strong on subtlety, Auntie threatened, "Wave, or you won't make it past tonight."

Though he hadn't been particularly afraid of her before, I suppose the comical incident had put him in a good mood.

"You could have said please," Clark pretended to grumble, but since Auntie stopped her threats, I suppose he'd given in and begun waving.

With the camera lens in front of me, I froze. My stomach tightened as I knew I was going to fail Auntie after all.

Then I remembered what Auntie had said about roles and performances. What would Norm have done if he had had this chance in the spotlight? And then I had a brainstorm on how to salvage this disaster. "Let go, Auntie," I whispered in Chinese. "I'm okay. You remember the routine from *Hold That Tiger Lil?*"

"Do I, kiddo? Who do you think taught Fred Astaire

to dance?" Under her breath, she began to count. "And a one and a two."

I did a credible imitation considering I had just been a one-girl demolition derby and was still strapped inside a jar and trying to recall the steps to a buck and wing.

Her shoes scraping on the asphalt, Auntie danced along with me. Perky, I reminded myself. You may be dented, but you're still ready to help the sore and afflicted. As I danced, though, I could feel all the aches and bruises; and no one would ever mistake me for Ginger Rogers. Still, when I heard the smattering of applause, it all almost seemed worthwhile.

Through the eye slits, I could see the bright lights of a big portable camera on us. They were so bright that I had to squint.

"And it's none other than Tiger Lil," I heard the reporter say. I recognized the voice. It belonged to one of the pretty Asian reporters on one of the news shows. "Quite a stunt, Tiger Lil," the reporter went on.

"Well, it wasn't planned, but then accidents never are," Auntie said smoothly. "That's why everyone needs a jar of Lion Salve at home."

I stood perkily while Auntie finished getting in a plug for her client. At least for her, the incident was worth a hundred thou to her client. Or whatever the cost of a minute's airtime was.

Next to me, Clark whispered, "Are you okay in there?" I think it amused him not to be in the spotlight for once.

I knew plenty of girls who would be asking me about my conversation with Clark. "It's nothing that a hot bubble bath couldn't cure," I whispered back.

"Not the salve?" he teased.

"I'd rather be dumped in sheep dip," I whispered back.

"It couldn't smell any worse," he agreed.

Then the camera lights went off. I could hear one of the parade marshals calling to the units to start up again. Auntie was jubilant as she hugged the jar. "I owe you a scoop of ginger ice cream."

"Are you kidding? You don't get off that cheap. It's going to cost you a banana split at least," I said.

"You can have ten," Auntie said cheerfully, getting carried away. "Twenty in fact." She helped turn me around so we could rejoin our parade unit. "You were fabulous. What a trouper. You saw that spotlight and you grabbed it."

The praise from her made me feel ten feet tall, and I almost bounced as I walked.

"Twenty banana splits and she won't be able to get out of the jar," Clark said, laughing. He reminded me a lot of Chris—and I didn't mean that as a compliment. "You got style, ma'am," he said respectfully to Auntie. "But if you were famous, how come I never heard of you?" The challenge was unmistakable in his voice.

I leaped indignantly to her defense. "Where've you been? She's Tiger Lil, the international star of stage and screen," I bragged. I could have gone on for an hour, but

I kept the summary short—to five minutes of highlights.

By the time I was finished, Clark sounded a little starstruck himself. "She's a pioneer. I don't know how I could have missed all that."

As we started back to the float, the streetlamps snapped on and I saw the light glint from something on the ground. It shone like a small round rainbow in the light of the streetlamps. Had I found a pearl? I hadn't seen the outcome when I had collided with Auntie and the Powell Street Boy. However, he'd been holding both ends of the necklace, so if the necklace had snapped, he might have been able to hold on to most of the pearls. But maybe this one had come off.

The trouble was that the costume brought me up short, so I could not reach the pearl with my hands. Of course, the moment I tried to position myself above it, the large jar costume cut off my view. I had to approximate where it was, hovering like a flying saucer while I slipped off one cloth shoe. Groping, I swept my foot slowly in widening arcs until I felt something round and hard and big as a marble. Gently, I eased my foot over it until my toes could curl around it. Then I raised my foot to where my fingers could get it.

Tilting the jar so that the streetlight could come through the eyeslits, I looked at what was in my hand. I was sure I was holding a solitary Goblin Pearl. "Auntie," I called.

"Over here," Auntie said to my left.

Through the eye slits, I saw Auntie standing over a

81

jar on its knees in the street. I assumed it was poor Norm exhausted from trying to run inside the costume. It was a shame, in a way, that it couldn't have been him on camera rather than me.

"Auntie," I said, trying to tell her I had the pearl.

"Not now, kiddo," Auntie said to me as she bent over Norm. "You okay?"

She and Chris helped Norm struggle awkwardly to his feet. "Yeah," he panted. "It's just hard to breathe in these things."

"They ought to come with air-conditioning," I sympathized.

He turned to me. "You did good, kid. I saw you shuffling off to Buffalo."

"I just followed your advice," I admitted truthfully.

"Yeah?" Though Norm was still wheezing, my words put a new strut into his walk as we headed back toward the float—even if Alan Alda wasn't supposed to strut.

Ahead of us, the drum corps had picked up their instruments and re-formed in even ranks. When they saw us coming, they parted silently to either side like the waves of the Red Sea, and from their dark glares as we passed, I didn't think I ought to expect any Christmas cards this year. In fact, if I hadn't been with Clark, I think someone might have tried to take revenge by tripping me.

The one I really felt sorry for, though, was Mrs. Wong. The Powell Street Boys had won after all.

# CHAPTER TEN

A Chinese policeman, Officer Quan, took our reports. He was dressed in a yellow raincoat, and plastic protected his cap against the expected rain. There really wasn't a lot to tell because the thief had a mask on.

As Auntie and I finished, Tiffany eased off the float and onto the street. Pointing, she began to charge toward me. "You—" she said, and pointed at me. "You're the cause of this, you clumsy oaf. He got away because of you! We saw everything from on top of the float." She pulled at the sleeve of the policeman who was interviewing me. "I want it on record just in case we sue her."

Mrs. Wong calmed Tiffany down. "The insurance company can do that if they want. I've just reported the theft to them." She nodded to a nearby pay phone.

"I got one of them back," I said.

"You what?" Mrs. Wong said.

Realizing I couldn't hand it to her, I pitched it at her feet. "It was on the street."

Mrs. Wong continued to stare at it as if I had just spit at her toes. Eyes widening, she skipped backward a step. "What kind of joke is this?"

Officer Quan squatted and picked it up. "You mean this isn't a Goblin Pearl?"

"Of course not," Mrs. Wong said. "It must be from some fake souvenier necklace."

Auntie looked surprised and shook her head. "I've never seen such a good fake."

"Then here's a souvenir." Officer Quan handed it back to me through one of my eye slits.

"Thanks." It would look neat sewn to the top of my black-and-gold beret, and I stowed it carefully away in my pants pocket.

After that, the parade was almost anticlimactic, and when we got to the end, I finally got to take off my costume. As I felt my flushed, sweaty face emerge into the cool air, I took a deep breath. "Now I know how a sardine feels."

All the other actors were gasping like fish as they freed themselves from their costumes. Norm, it turned out, was a pleasant-faced man with blond hair. "You're a chip off the old block," he said.

"Blockhead, you mean." Auntie threaded her way among the discarded jars, which lay like gigantic extracted molars, and wrapped her arms around me. "You really saved the day, kiddo." I could tell she was proud.

"I didn't save the pearls though," I said.

"No, but you tried," she said.

That meant a lot to me. "It was nothing," I said modestly, and then, as a new thought occurred to me, I grew alarmed. What if she drafted me for her other projects? "Really," I said with more sincerity this time, "it was nothing. Just forget it."

"Well, you're one lady I won't forget," Clark said to Auntie. "Have you got a card?"

"Have I got a card." Auntie chuckled as she dug a hand into her huge bag and pulled out a dozen, peeling off one to hand to him. "Call me anytime, kiddo."

"I will," Clark promised, and raised the card in a kind of salute before he tapped it against his forehead.

Mr. Soo came up then, holding both thumbs up. "You were so brave," he said in English. "You did well." He shook my hand and then Auntie's. "But where is Miss Lion Salve?"

"They skipped out like their dresses were on fire," Clark said.

"They're probably upset about the theft," Auntie said sympathetically.

"Such a terrible thing to happen to such a brave lady," Mr. Soo agreed. "But I think we have to carry on."

"I'm sure the cops will catch the thief," Clark said, and raised his hand. "Well, so long. I've got to catch the red-eye back to L.A."

"You can't stay for the banquet?" Mr. Soo asked sadly.

"Shooting begins at seven tomorrow morning." Clark waved to everyone as he left.

Mr. Soo turned then to the actors and clapped his hands together as he beamed at them. "I think we all have to make the best of a terrible evening. You're all invited to the banquet. Please join me."

Now that the Powell Street Boys had struck and gone, everyone felt safe, and at the mention of free food, the actors gave a boisterous, rousing cheer while Mr. Soo basked in their happiness. Between Chris and the actors, I just hoped the restaurant had made enough food.

I began to hear hundreds of firecrackers going off behind us, so loud it sounded like World War Three. They were probably setting them off for the climax of the parade as the dragon danced for the camera. The noise ought to have been enough to chase the goblins right out of town. For once, the cops, who were everywhere, were letting people shoot them off.

The first raindrops began to fall as we walked down to the post-parade Lion Salve celebration, and we heard a rumble that was definitely thunder.

However, nothing could ruin the mood. The actors, anticipating a good meal, were as rowdy as children. Along the way, they made up chants to which we could march. Mr. Soo played along by waving his arms like a symphony conductor.

"Give me an 'L'," Norman shouted.

"L," everyone yelled back.

"Let them hear it over in Oakland," Auntie exhorted them.

"L!" they shouted even louder.

At the final "E," a bolt of lightning flashed overhead and thunder boomed. Everyone picked up the pace, trying to reach the restaurant before the light rainfall changed to a deluge.

I slipped over to Auntie. "Mr. Soo seems pretty happy right now. Maybe he's ready to invest in a movie."

"Or other things," Auntie muttered, more to herself than to me.

I remembered the other projects she had described on the first day she had arrived. "What things? Maybe a play?" I speculated eagerly.

"You never know, kiddo." With a chuckle, Auntie plunged in among the other actors, leaving me feeling curious and frustrated.

The banquet was held at a fancy eatery, the Ciao Chow, a couple blocks from Chinatown over on Battery Street. It was funny to see a Chinese restaurant in the lower part of a twenty-story high-rise. All around it, the steel and glass towers of the business district shut out the night sky.

I glanced at the menu hung up against one window and whistled at the prices. "You could feed a family of four for what one dish costs here." And I glanced at the list of some of the dishes. They would have had most of the old-timers on Grant Avenue scratching their heads in puzzlement. "Whoever heard of ravioli with ground duck and Chinese sausage?"

"Ain'cha got cul-cha?" Auntie asked in a Brooklyn

accent, and then in lower voice, she explained. "This is what they call Nouvelle Chinese cuisine, kiddo. It's the latest in thing. I'm angling to land them as clients."

A tall American in a tan suit with broad, padded shoulders intercepted us, blocking our path with a pair of red, leather-bound menus in his hand. "Can I help you?" He had a warm, velvety voice that could have sold anything on television.

"We're here for the Lion Salve party," Auntie said. "I'm Lil Leung."

The man smiled and thrust out his free hand. "I'm Morgan Fisher. We spoke on the phone." He was Barry's father!

Auntie put her fists on her hips and surveyed him. "So you're Ann's husband."

He slapped the menus against his palm. "Guilty." He used the menus to point to a flight of steel steps rising to a second floor. "Many of your party have already arrived."

"They probably didn't even go to the parade but came straight here."

"They probably figured it was safer here," I said.

Mr. Fisher turned his sunny smile toward me and beamed. "And your name, miss?"

Barry definitely had gotten his father's build and hair color, but he didn't have his father's sociability. Even as I wondered what had made my teammate so shy, I said, "I'm Lily Lew."

Mr. Fisher's smile broadened. "I'm pleased to meet

you finally. Barry's always talking about you."

I didn't think Barry talked about anything but the martial arts or maybe some computer game he and Akeem played. "He does?"

"According to him, the sun sets where you say it does." Mr. Fisher turned toward the stairs.

Auntie couldn't help nudging me. "I think you've got a boyfriend, kiddo."

I wasn't sure I wanted a boyfriend; and even if I did, I don't think I would have picked Barry. "Mr. Fisher must be mistaken."

Mr. Fisher's long legs had no trouble mounting the steps, but it was a little harder for Auntie and me. As we climbed the steps, Auntie whispered to me, "Wish me luck, kiddo. Let's hope Mr. Soo thinks he's gotten his money's worth."

I squeezed Auntie's arm. "Good luck."

Mr. Soo said from behind us, "Where are Mrs. Wong and Tiffany?"

Auntie set her hand beneath his elbow and started to guide him up the stairs. "They may still be trying to recover from the theft. We've got other guests. As you said, we have to make the best of things."

Mr. Fisher was waiting for us at the top. "I hope everything is to your liking," he said with a bow.

When we joined him, I saw that a long, low buffet table had been set out on the mezzanine. There were ten tables set up along the walls where people could sit, and an open space in the center where people could mingle.

Mr. Soo spread his hands. "How wonderful."

Mom and Dad were already at the buffet table, sampling the dim sum that had been laid out. Mom waved excitedly to me. "Hey, come on and meet someone. She's almost as famous as Auntie."

A Chinese woman in a chef's hat and white jacket shrugged modestly. "My cooking show is only on cable."

"Ann Fisher," Auntie said, steering Mr. Soo over. "Mr. Soo, let me introduce you to one of the rising young stars not only in Chinatown but in the city's culinary circles. And that's saying something."

"Ooo, that looks interesting," Mom said, examining something.

"I'll be offended if you don't try the hundred-day-old eggs in a basket," Mrs. Fisher said to Mom. Mom had a way of making friends instantly; but then so, obviously, did Mrs. Fisher. For sociability, she was a good match for her husband. Barry was nothing like either parent.

Hundred-day-old eggs were eggs that had been coated in clay and left to age until the yolks had turned a lovely deep violet. These yolks, though, looked a kind of yucky green, but they were still tasty. The eggs had been sliced and set in baskets made from fried, crunchy noodles.

Auntie whispered to me, "You go ahead, kiddo. I've got to check on things."

Auntie began to work the rest of the room with her client, Mr. Soo. Or maybe I should say the room worked them, because there was a big rush toward Auntie and Mr. Soo to thank them for the party.

"How lovely a repast! What a splendid way to end the festivities," said a well-dressed man with black horn-rimmed glasses. His ears stuck out almost perpendicular to his head.

"Something's up," Dad muttered to Mom. "Arthur's always around whenever there's a big deal going on."

"He does have a nose for money," Mom agreed.

Dad plucked his lip. "I overheard someone saying that Mr. Soo was planning to move his company head-quarters here from Hong Kong. This trip is kind of a scouting expedition."

Mom began calculating in her head. She let out a low whistle. "A company headquarters. He'll need a lot of square footage."

The move probably meant a lot of money for Auntie as well, if Mr. Soo asked her to handle more publicity for him. Maybe he'd even finance her movie.

With difficulty, Auntie disentangled Mr. Soo from Arthur's octopuslike grip and guided him away to a group of taller Chinese with round, pale faces. In their center was a tall man with thinning hair, wearing an elegant gray suit. Acting as spokesman, he first dipped his head and then held out his hand. "You've put us to shame, Mr. Soo. It's we who should have given the banquet, since you're the visitor."

Curious, I leaned over and whispered to Dad, "Who's that?"

He put his hand on mine and shoved it down. "Don't point. It's rude."

From Auntie's and Mr. Soo's attitudes, I gathered he must be some V.I.P. "So is he a big shot?"

"Very big," Dad confirmed. "That's the son of the famous architect S. Z. Li. He and his father design buildings all around the world. His father came here over fifty years ago from Taiwan, and the son was born here. But they've always maintained strong ties with Taiwan. Most of his friends there represent huge Taiwanese companies."

"No kidding." I watched Mr. Li more closely. He moved and spoke in a quiet, self-assured way that assumed people would defer.

"Chinatown's been so kind, Mr. Li." Mr. Soo beamed pleasantly. "This is just a little thank-you to a few of my new friends."

Mr. Li's eyes darted around the room. "I was wondering where Mrs. Wong was."

While Auntie and Mr. Soo narrated the capture and escape of the thief, and described Mrs. Wong's reactions, Mr. Li gulped down his drink and helped himself to more.

Mr. Soo saw me. "And then Miss Lily's niece tried to help her aunt catch the thief, but alas, it wasn't meant to be."

Technically, I had been more involved in the thief's escape than in his capture, but I was glad Mr. Soo had described it the way he had.

Auntie finished by saying, "That thief won't get far. Where can you fence something as big and noticeable as the Goblin Pearls?"

Arthur contemplated the fizzing bubbles in the bottom of the glass. "The loss is still a tragedy. Poor Mrs. Wong."

Mr. Li seemed to be feeling just as bad as Arthur. "It's a loss to us as a people," he said, pivoting on his heel.

"Yes, yes, terrible," Mr. Soo agreed.

Everyone made sympathetic comments about Mrs. Wong, and then when Mr. Soo and Auntie finally moved off, I noticed that Mr. Li and his circle began to speak in a different dialect to one another. A woman gestured to her throat as if to a necklace and then pointed at Auntie and finally toward me.

I strained my ears to hear what they were saying, but I couldn't understand a word. "What are they talking?" I asked in exasperation. "Their Chinese sounds so different."

"It's Mandarin," Dad explained. "That's what they talk on Taiwan and on the mainland of China."

"And they'd say their dialect is the real Chinese," Chris said, snorting.

Frustrated, I turned toward him. "Well, what do we talk then?"

"Cantonese," Chris said, "from southern China. Or to be more specific, from Toisan, to the southwest of the city of Canton. And some of us speak it better than others," he added. It was a wisecrack aimed at my own inadequate Chinese.

As much as I hated to have to ask him for any kind

of information, Chris had been studying our roots. "So what does that mean for someone who doesn't know Chinese geography?"

Chris sighed in an annoyed way. "You know American geography, right?"

"A little," I said tentatively.

He rearranged some teacups that had been grouped in the middle around a teapot. "Well, Mr. Li is a northerner—picture it as someplace like New York. And our group comes from a place like Mississippi. Except our group has been sending people over here for four generations rather than one."

I remembered that Dad had said Mrs. Wong was from Hong Kong. "And people from Hong Kong?"

Chris scratched his chin. "Well, it's not exact, but geographically they're like people from Florida." He nodded to another group in the room. "There's a bunch of them there." Though the men wore normal, drab business suits, the women were heavily into sequins and bows and frills and wild colors.

"With the changes in the immigration laws," Chris explained, "there's a lot more Chinese trying to come here from Hong Kong. Especially now that the mainland's going to take over again, they're scared and running for America."

It's funny, but I had been going to gatherings like this in Chinatown all my life, but I had never paid attention to them before this. If you had asked me who was present, I would have said a bunch of Chinese.

Tonight, people all over the room seemed to be discussing the theft, following two parallel tracks: On the one hand, everybody felt sorry for Mrs. Wong, who had tried to defy the Powell Street Boys; and on the other hand, everyone wondered what could be done about such brazen thieves.

Mr. Soo finally grabbed a cup of tea from a table. "May I have your attention, everybody?"

However, his voice didn't carry very far, so I picked up a spoon that lay on the table and tapped it against a glass of water. As the bell-like tones rang through the room, heads turned until they settled on Mr. Soo.

When he had everyone's eyes on him, he raised his teacup. "I want to toast the woman who saved the parade. I don't know who else could have pulled it off in the face of such calamities."

Somewhere in the room, there was a clink as someone reached for a teacup. And then I heard another clink. And another. Everywhere in the room, people were getting teacups or glasses of water. When everyone had something, Mr. Soo beamed at Auntie. "To Tiger Lil. I want you to handle all my publicity from now on."

"I do have projects," Auntie hinted vaguely. I held my breath, waiting for her to name her Tiger Lil movie.

"When you have time in between," Mr. Soo pressed her.

I sagged in my seat, because he wanted to stay rooted in his herbal salve business. I thought Auntie would be disappointed, but she was too good an actor to show it.

Mom's eyes widened, though, as she began to scheme. "I've got room at the back of the beauty parlor. Auntie could set up a desk there."

Dad waved a hand around the room. "She should get plenty of business after tonight."

In the meantime, Auntie was speaking with formal modesty. "I don't know if I'm up to it."

"Of course, you are," Mr. Soo insisted. "Let's hear no more about it."

"I'd be honored," Auntie replied.

"The honor is mine," Mr. Soo answered. All over the room, people began raising their cups and glasses in Auntie's honor again. And when Mr. Li lifted his glass, his whole group did. And then one by one, everyone began to salute Auntie.

Suddenly I was glad for Auntie. In that room with all these rich people around, Mr. Soo's endorsement was as good as a bar of gold. Even if Mr. Soo didn't want to invest in her movie, maybe one of them would.

Tiger Lil would live on.

# CHAPTER ELEVEN

A t that moment, Mr. Soo turned and called out loudly, "Where are you going, Mrs. Wong? People are asking about you."

One look at Mrs. Wong and I understood why she hadn't wanted to call attention to herself. She stood in the center of the room, her face wet and her mascara running—she looked like a raccoon. Behind her stood a sullen Tiffany, who sagged nearly as much as her hairdo. It seemed like the final indignity after the theft, and I really began to feel sorry for her.

Mrs. Wong smiled nervously. "Oh, are they?" Though she spoke to Mr. Soo, her eyes roved around the room until they settled on Auntie; and she gave Auntie what Daniel, my Hawaiian friend, would have called "stink eye." Mrs. Wong had neither forgiven nor forgotten. I was afraid that not only would there be a lawsuit, but this was the start of a nasty Chinatown-style feud.

Tiffany slumped beside her mother like a water-logged flower. Her eyes, though, scanned the room until she found me. With a jolt, I realized she blamed me for helping the thief escape. Tugging at her mother's sleeve, she pointed at me.

Heading for the stairs, Mrs. Wong smiled nervously. "I'll be back in a moment."

Mr. Soo kept flapping his hand as if his wrist were a spool and he was reeling them in with an invisible thread. "It can wait. Drink something hot first."

Mrs. Wong placed a hand beneath her throat. "No, this evening has been too much for me. I really shouldn't have tried to come here." She grasped at her daughter's shoulder. "Tiffany, take me home."

Tiffany dipped dangerously under the weight. "But—"

"Take me home," Mrs. Wong insisted.

However, the Hong Kong contingent immediately flocked around Mrs. Wong to comfort her. Mrs. Wong pushed at the crush of well-wishers. "Please, I feel faint. I must have air."

Suddenly Norm's voice carried up the staircase. "Hey, we made the newscast. Hurry up and come down to the bar." I guess he had drifted down there after eating upstairs.

I lost sight of the Wongs in the general surge toward the stairs and into the bar. The bar was lit by red bulbs that made the dragons carved on the wall appear lurid. A television was suspended by chains from the ceiling so everyone could see. An advertisement for tires was running at the moment. I suppose there had been some teaser that had warned everyone about the parade before the station had cut to the commercial break.

As the others snaked inside the bar, I stopped by the doorway with Auntie and Chris. "Four thousand years of culture just to push a cheap medicine," he grumbled.

"Will you get off your high horse," I grunted.

He grinned at me scornfully. "What would you know about it? You quit Chinese school after a month."

"The teachers were too strict." I shrugged.

"Or are you ashamed?" he demanded.

I defended myself. "I've lived in or near Chinatown all my life."

"And never given your heritage a thought."

I wanted to protest that wasn't true, but then I thought about the crowd at the buffet. There had been all those different groups up there—like the colors in the rainbow—but I was like someone who was seeing only black and white. For once in my life, I thought I might have to agree with Chris.

Fortunately, the commercial came to an end at that moment, and Norm called loudly for quiet. As the bar fell silent, the screen went dark, and the next moment a talking head appeared. She was the reporter who had filmed us before.

She stared straight at us as she intoned, "Thieves struck Chinatown once again, robbing H. T. Wong of the fabled Goblin Pearls."

The screen cut to a close-up of Supervisor Macek, who basically said "I told you so," and then returned to the reporter. Looking at the camera, she spoke with mock solemnity. "Further tragedy almost struck the Chinese New Year's parade." I waited, expecting her to talk about the theft of the Goblin Pearls. Instead, she swung her head to face a different camera. "A jar of Lion Salve got loose, terrifying dozens."

There was a picture of me rolling through the startled band before they cut back to the reporter. "Fortunately, no one was injured."

The camera pulled back to show an anchor sitting behind a desk. "And no one slipped on all that salve?"

"No," the reporter deadpanned, "but two potholes were healed. City officials are studying the possibility of using salve in other contexts."

As they cut to the weather, I gave a disappointed groan. "A joke. They turned the whole thing into a joke."

Auntie stared at the television. "At least they got the name of the product right."

A laughing man shouted across the bar, "Hey, Tiger Lil, who was in the jar?"

"Yeah, who?" a woman yelled from a distant corner.

As others began to badger Auntie loudly into revealing my identity, I decided to beat a hasty retreat. Chris was quite capable of pointing me out to the room—and by extension, all of Chinatown. " 'Scuse me. I have to go to the ladies' room."

"Coward," Chris sneered.

I tried to catch one of the tuxedoed waiters, but they were more slippery than a USC tailback. Then I saw an elderly Chinese man in a white T-shirt and slacks shuffling along.

"The rest room?" I asked him in Chinese.

He gave a barely noticeable bob of his head. "This way." Slowly he trundled the bucket ahead of him down a dim passageway off the bar.

I hesitated, since the only light came from the bar's lights, but as his bony shoulders disappeared into the dark, I plunged after him.

When he heard me following him, he didn't look around as he asked, "Where are you from?"

"First City," I said in Chinese, meaning San Francisco.

I saw the back of his head shake back and forth. "I meant your family." He added, "In the Middle Kingdom." By Middle Kingdom, he meant China.

Mom and Dad had been born here too, and they had never sat me down to talk about the family history. Desperately I tried to recall bits of past conversation between Dad and Mom. "Toisan," I said. "I think."

"You have the accent of a country hick," he muttered.

"Hey," I protested.

He looked over his shoulder and seemed mildly amused that I had been offended. "It's okay. I'm a hick too."

It was hard to keep from treading on his heels, he

was moving so slowly. Then he moved to one side of the passageway so I could join him.

As I slid in next to him, he looked ahead again. "What does your father do?"

"He work . . ." I paused because I didn't know the Chinese words for silicon chips. "He make thing you use in . . ." I didn't know the word for computer either.

The farther we went, the darker it seemed to get. If he hadn't been wearing such light clothes, I might have lost sight of him. "You talk like a three-year-old," he scolded me. "But you're a big girl. Learn enough Chinese to talk like one."

I was beginning to regret that I hadn't tackled an English-speaking waiter. "Yes, sir."

"Is your father rich?" he asked.

I stopped dead. "I don't think that's any of your business."

He let out a loud laugh. "You are native born," he said, and trundled on.

I thought of a dozen angry retorts centering on the fact that we were in America and not China; but then I figured we were close enough to Chinatown to count. And I'd actually heard enough conversations between my parents and old-timers during which the old-timers had asked them personal questions too. I had never understood why my parents hadn't gotten mad, the way they would have if Americans had asked those questions.

Tonight, though, I had learned a few things first-hand about what status and family meant. I could see why it was important to establish those things quickly. Maybe the old-timer hadn't meant to be insulting.

I hurried down the passageway until I reached its end. In the dim light, I made out three doors—none of them labeled.

The elderly Chinese opened the middle door to reveal brooms, mops, rolls of paper towels and so on. He stopped in the middle of rolling the bucket into the broom closet to watch me with amusement.

Taking a guess, I pulled gently at the door with the carving of the woman and peeked inside.

Filling one wall were sinks of pink marble with golden fixtures, but what impressed me the most was that the towel dispensers were also of pink marble.

"Lucky guess, native born," the old man teased as he began to shut the broom closet door.

"I knew it," I grumbled. Until tonight, I might have thought of him as just a jerk, but that was because I assumed all Chinese Americans were the same and ought to be like me. Now I realized we came in all sizes and types. So I forced myself to add, "Thank you."

"You're welcome," he said, sounding startled as the door closed.

Inside the rest room, each stall was metal and colored pink to match the sinks. Opening the first, I was just starting to go in when the lights went off. My first thought was that the power had gone out, but suddenly

I heard heavy steps coming straight toward me. Suddenly I caught a whiff of cigar smoke again.

Wheeling around, I groped at the cold smoothness of the stall door until I found the bolt. I shot it just in time as a body thumped against the door.

"Auntie," I shouted. "Help, Auntie!"

"Your aunt can't help you," someone rasped. "I want the pearl." Rationally I knew it was only a man trying to disguise his voice by pitching it low, but he made it sound like a goblin's.

"It's just a fake," I said, remembering Mrs. Wong's reaction.

"It belongs to me. I want it," the goblin growled.

Though I was shaking with fear in the dark, I managed to climb onto the toilet seat. Then I stretched my hands out until I grasped the top of one stall side.

Beneath me I could hear the goblin panting—in the dark that was the only way my fearful imagination could conceive of him. He must have slid underneath the stall door.

In a panic, I started to pull myself up when his hand brushed my foot. For the first time in my life, I began to wish I'd been more diligent about rope climbing in P.E. class. The panic, though, got the adrenaline rushing through me, and I hoisted myself up so that my stomach was on top of the stall.

From below came grunts, and then his hand found my ankle. I kicked down hard with my free foot and connected with something heavy. He still held on to me

104

tightly. "Here's your pearl," I said, and threw a sourball I had in my pocket. Suddenly the hand released me and I pulled myself over.

The memory of his grip burned at my ankle, lending me speed. I crashed through the door and out into the hall. My momentum carried me into the opposite wall and I bounced off. Straightening, I headed right for the old-timer's broom closet.

I jerked the plain door open and found the old-timer's bucket. Seizing the mop handle, I yanked it from the bucket so hard that the bucket rocked on its wheels and water splashed all over me from the mop head. I didn't care. With a twist of my wrist, I twirled it so that it was horizontal like a spear. Back to the women's rest room I darted, trailing water behind me.

To my alarm, I saw the door with the woman begin to open. Frantically I flung myself at it. Even though I was leaning all my weight against the door, it still started to give way before the goblin on the other side.

"Help," I called, but there was too much noise in the bar for anyone to hear me. If I was going to capture the goblin, I would have to do it myself.

I dug my feet into the carpet, then set my free hand and my shoulder against the cold surface. Desperately I began to shove at the door with all my strength. Though I couldn't move it back toward the frame, I kept it from swinging open any wider.

Suddenly the door swung closed all on its own. As I started to fall, I realized the goblin must have stepped back. I still had the mop in my hand, and I used it to shove myself upright just in time.

"You're tricky," I said triumphantly, "but you fooled yourself."

With the door even with the frame, I started to bring up the mop handle. Before I could trap him, though, the door banged into me as if the goblin had thrown himself at it like a battering ram. The goblin must have turned on the light in the women's room again, because there was a flash of light like a lightning bolt as the door opened a couple of inches.

Whirling around, I set my back against the door and grimly braced my feet. As I struggled to shut the door, I could hear the goblin's muffled squeals and snorts from within as he fought to open it.

"Give me the pearl!" he kept insisting.

"N-never," I said, my voice vibrating under the force of the goblin's blows. Operating as a human barricade was hard work.

Suddenly I had an idea, and I fished the pearl out of my pocket with my free hand. "H-here," I said, and threw it through the crack between the open door and the frame. I heard it rattle as it rolled across the tiles, and suddenly the door shut as the goblin turned to pursue it.

I'd been ready this time, so I kept my balance. Pivoting, I slipped the handle through the door handle of the women's room door, and then I slid it through the handle on the broom closet door.

"Got you." I sighed with relief.

When the goblin threw himself at the door, it opened an inch and then stopped, checked by the mop handle.

Human fingers, rather than claws, reached for the shaft. The light from the women's room flashed off a large, heavy gold ring.

"Help, police," I shouted again as I stood on one leg. Taking my shoe from my free foot, I stared down at the mop handle and then swung my shoe down hard on the fingers that were trying to slide the shaft from the door handle. There was a very humanlike yell rather than an unearthly screech.

Reassured that I was dealing with a human rather than a supernatural prowler, I hopped into the restaurant on the foot that was still shod. Mr. Fisher was busy tallying up the receipts at the cash register while Mrs. Fisher and Auntie stood nearby chatting.

"Auntie, help," I panted.

"There you are. I've been looking all over for you." Auntie turned around, but when she took in my sweaty face, her eyes widened, "What's going on, kiddo?"

"Someone just attacked me." I almost said "goblin," but I stopped myself in time. "I caught him in the ladies' rest room."

"I'll teach him a lesson," Auntie said angrily. Rolling up her sleeves, she plunged down the passageway.

Mrs. Fisher signed to her husband. "Morgan," she said, "will you come with me?" Without checking to see if he was with her, she plunged down the dim passageway. Her white chef's hat bobbed like a white mushroom.

Limping, I followed them down the passageway back to the rest rooms, not any too eager to renew my acquaintance with the goblin. In one hand Auntie was holding a shoe like a club while her other hand grasped the mop handle.

"Auntie, don't pull the mop handle away," I shouted in warning. "Wait for the police."

Mrs. Fisher found a switch hidden by a large vase on a narrow table and flicked it, flooding the passageway with light. "Better take care of it, Morgan."

It wasn't too long before a restaurant employee led two uniformed cops—Officer Quan, who had taken our statements at the parade, and a redheaded white woman—to us. Their coats and caps were beaded with raindrops. Trailing behind them was a curious Norm.

"We'll take over," the woman said, motioning us to the side.

Officer Quan stared at the door. "Geez, it's a women's room. You go, Siezmanski."

"You're too squeamish." When we were clear, she spread her feet and drew her revolver. When I glanced at Auntie, I saw her studying the cops as if memorizing their movements for a future role.

At Officer Siezmanski's nod, Officer Quan drew the shaft from the door handles. "Come out with your hands up," Officer Siezmanski ordered in a loud voice.

When there was no answer, she nodded again to her partner, who swung the door open. Officer Siezmanski leaped into the women's room, pivoting this way and that with her gun. She straightened. "The prowler's gone," she said.

We probably should have stayed outside, but our curiosity drew us in after the second cop as he entered. "Flew the coop," Siezmanski said, and pointed.

An icy breeze blew through the open window on the wall, and I could see the bars had been shoved aside by someone with superhuman strength.

fficer Quan, though, seemed more impressed by the decor than by the feat of supernatural strength.

"I've never been in a ladies' room before," he said admiringly as he turned in a slow circle. "Is the men's room this nice?"

"I doubt it," Norm said amiably, turning from the window. "Look at what I found."

Quan and Siezmanski seemed to notice Norm for the first time. Siezmanski used the brim of her cap to shove it back on her head. "Just who are you, anyway?"

Norm dug his wallet from his pocket and handed a card to her. His voice became level and very professional. "Acting is just a hobby. I'm an Assistant District Attorney."

My jaw was still open when Norm glanced at me. He winked. "You very rarely get actors to admit to their day jobs."

Siezmanski held it out to Quan after she finished

reading it. With more respect in her voice, she asked, "What did you find, sir?"

"Just this." Norm turned back to the window, and we all tried to squeeze in around him to see.

Norm pointed at the twisted window bars at the bottom of the window. "It's like I suspected—rusted."

Even though there was now a rational explanation for the window, I still felt uneasy. I couldn't shake the feeling that we were dealing with a goblin.

I almost felt as if I weren't in my body. It was somebody else they led up the steps and somebody else who sat down at a table on the mezzanine. Mr. Soo was thoroughly apologetic, as if the attack had been his fault. Dad and Mom were angry. Even Chris was indignant.

Mrs. Fisher got me a cup of tea and then stood beside me, with her hand protectively on my shoulder. I liked Barry's mother.

Most everyone in the Lion Salve party had returned to the mezzanine to retrieve their coats. I could feel them staring at me. When they tried to leave, though, Norm stopped them. "I'm afraid we may need all of you."

By twos and threes, Mr. Soo's other guests reluctantly began to sit down around the other tables. Ever the good host, Mr. Soo whispered something in Mrs. Fisher's ear.

"Paul, drinks and sodas for everyone," she said to a waiter, becoming the professional restaurateur again.

Fortunately, people did not have long to wait. A platoon of cops showed up right away. (I assumed Norm himself had called.) From the mezzanine, I could see some of them heading for the rest rooms with big metal boxes—I suppose to take fingerprints. The others, at Norm's direction, came upstairs to take statements.

Auntie and I gave ours to Siezmanski and Quan. When I got to the part about the pearl, I shook my head. "I don't see why he wanted it, though. At first, I thought it was a Goblin Pearl, but Mrs. Wong says it wasn't."

"It looked like the real thing to me. I was surprised when she said it wasn't. Don't you think it's odd that she didn't examine it closer?" Auntie asked. "If I'd lost something that precious, I would have."

Norm had been straddling a chair to one side, listening silently. He turned to Siezmanski and Quan. "This thief seemed to think it was real enough."

Even if the goblin had gotten what he wanted, I didn't like the idea of him being on the loose. I still remembered that scary chase in the dark.

Auntie hunched forward with a look that I remembered from *Tiger Lil to the Rescue*. "I thought something was funny when Clark spilled wine all over the necklace, but I couldn't put my finger on it until now."

I tried to remember. "But Mrs. Wong had a right to be angry."

"Yes, but she should have also been anxious about the pearls." Auntie plucked her lip. "Wine has acid, so it can dissolve pearls. She should have immediately tried to wash them off rather than tend to Tiffany's dress first."

I scratched my forehead. "But pearls are gems."

"They're organic gems, kiddo." Auntie held up a thumb and forefinger. "They begin with a grain of sand inside an oyster, and because that tiny grain of sand irritates the oyster, the oyster begins to coat it. Year by year the coating grows around the sand."

"Until you have a pearl," I said, finally realizing what she was getting at.

Auntie nodded. "It's not like a diamond, which is a stone. Wine can eat away at pearls. Mrs. Wong must have known that, but she wasn't worried."

"So maybe they weren't real!" I said.

Auntie nodded. "I doubt they were. A lot of the famous and rich don't wear their real jewelry. Instead, they wear expensive imitations. The real Goblin Pearls are probably someplace safe. The Wongs wouldn't risk damaging their precious treasure. But why is Mrs. Wong making believe the real pearls have been stolen? Unless that's what she wanted all along! Now it all makes sense!"

Norm ran a thumb across his lips. "So the Wongs used a fake string of pearls—after all, why risk the real pearls? Then they pretend that the real pearls are stolen in front of hundreds of witnesses, framing the Powell Street Boys for the crime. I bet they planned to collect the insurance money afterward and keep the real pearls hidden."

Auntie inclined her head toward me. "Only Lily here got hold of one of the fake pearls."

I was finally beginning to understand. "So it was the Wongs who came looking for me?"

Auntie settled back in her chair. "Yes. They had to get back the fake."

"But I offered it to her back at the parade," I said.

"When a policeman was there," Auntie pointed out. "If she had said it was hers, he would have taken it to dust for fingerprints, right, Norm?"

Norm rose and stretched his long frame. "We would have discovered that it was a fake. The whole scam would have fallen apart. So she had to wait till later."

Auntie nodded. "So she found her confederate and worked out what to do. Then she came here to locate you, Lily. She might have been able to sneak in and out if it hadn't been for the sharp eyes of Mr. Soo."

I shivered. That made her sound so deliberate and coldblooded. "And I thought she was so heroic."

"It's just as well you gave him what he wanted." Norm slid his chair under the table. "All in all, it's been quite an evening."

"That's an understatement," Auntie said as she got up. "You're going to get a lot of work from tonight."

Norm rubbed his head regretfully. "And a lot less time for acting."

"Are you finished, sir?" Quan asked him.

"Yes," Norm said, still looking unhappy. "It's time to send someone to pay a visit to the Wongs. We can't prove any of this, and we have no proof that the real pearls weren't stolen. She might get away with it after all." Then Norm turned to Auntie and me. "Well, that's it. You're free to go. My job is just starting."

Arm in arm, we turned to Mrs. Fisher, who had unbuttoned her coat and was sitting in a chair sipping a glass of wine. "Mrs. Fisher, do you know where Mr. Soo is?"

"He paid the bill and left," Mrs. Fisher said. "Didn't he talk to you?"

Auntie's shoulders sagged as if she were suddenly tired. "Did he seem angry?"

"Why would he be angry?" I asked.

"In just a few hours, his company has been involved in a theft and an assault," Auntie said. "This fiasco could cause him to lose face—not exactly the way you want to launch your product in America."

"He just seemed to be in a hurry," Mrs. Fisher said. "I guess it slipped his mind."

"Oh," Auntie said in a small voice. "I guess it did."

I felt even worse when Norm started to swear at one of the officers. "What do you mean there's no one there?"

The policeman shrugged as he held a radio in his hand. "They don't answer the doorbell or the phone, sir. And the neighbors say they saw them jump in a car and leave just before the patrol car got there."

Norm swore again. "Well, looks like the Wongs aren't taking any more chances. I better call on Judge Tierney and get a search warrant. In the meantime, put out an APB." Norm waved us over when he saw us. "Lily, can you help us with a description?"

"I never saw Mr. Wong, but we know Mrs. Wong and Tiffany," Auntie said, and gave the policeman an accurate portrayal of the two.

As we left, I told Auntie what Linda had told me about the Wongs' connection to the Happy Fortune. "The Wongs owe her mother and her friends three months' wages."

"Poor Linda." Auntie sighed. "Her mother's back pay is probably heading toward South America right now."

Yes, poor Linda. And poor Auntie too. It'd been a disaster for everyone.

# CHAPTER THIRTEEN

All day Sunday Mom and Dad took turns coddling me. Even Chris lent a hand—much to my surprise. As he growled to me, "I'm the only one who can pick on you. Nobody else can."

However, all their spoiling only made me feel more uncomfortable. I kept thinking about Linda and Auntie. What would they do now?

The air was so humid that no matter how I tried to lie in my bed, I felt wet and clammy. And outside my window, I saw the streets were just as miserable, with a drizzle that deposited little beads of rain all day long on the glass.

Finally, between my worries and the weather, I couldn't take it anymore, so I rolled out of bed and looked across the hallway.

Through the closed study door, I heard Auntie talking on the telephone. "Oh." There was disappointment in her voice. After a pause, I could hear her putting on a brave front again. "Naw, don't worry about me, Artie." Artie was her agent and one of her oldest and dearest friends. "I didn't really want to come back. It's great here. Lots of business opportunities." She gave a little laugh. "Yeah. Give me a call when you're up in the city." From her voice, I thought she doubted it would ever happen. "Yeah, 'bye."

To hear her talk to Mom and my friends, you'd think her career had been an elevator that had only gone upward. This was the first hint that it was otherwise. I guess if a career could go up like an elevator, it could also go down. Maybe there had been more at stake last night than I had realized. And Mr. Soo had left. . . .

Tiptoeing across the hallway, I knocked softly at the door. "Auntie?"

She made some reply that was muffled by the door. I decided it was an invitation to enter.

Auntie waved a tissue at me. "I said wait a moment."

"I . . . I misheard you," I stammered as I held on to the doorknob.

"I got this darn hay fever, you know. Makes my eyes water like Niagara Falls."

"Sure," I said, wanting to let her save face. "Sorry, Auntie."

She wiped hastily at her eyes and then smiled bravely. "It's okay, kiddo. I should've put a Do Not Disturb sign on the doorknob."

I twisted my hand first one way on the doorknob and then the other. Down below, a doorbell rang. "No, not for that. For not getting Mr. Soo to back your movie. You must feel awful."

"Them's the breaks. It could be worse. Think about Linda's family." Impulsively Auntie spread out her arms. "Come here, kiddo."

Closing the door, I went over to the bed, where Auntie gave me a bear hug. "What are you going to do now?"

"Oh"—Auntie waved a hand airily—"my agent says there's plenty of projects for me."

Auntie was so good an actor that I would have believed her if I hadn't overheard her phone conversation. "I heard part of what you said to Artie."

Miffed, Auntie tugged one of my earlobes. "I thought loud rock music had destroyed your generation's eardrums."

I wasn't about to let her joke her way out of this the way she usually did. "What will you do?" I demanded anxiously.

Auntie patted me on the cheek. "Don't worry about me, kiddo. Tiger Lil can take care of herself."

"Don't depend on Artie," I urged her. "Why don't you call up some of your famous friends? You know, the ones you took all those photos with."

"I wish I could, but the studio staged them for publicity, kiddo. The real stars wouldn't know me from Eve." Auntie chuckled like the joke was on her.

119

"But you told Mom and me and my classmates about all those parties and the premieres."

"I read about them in the fan mags like anyone else." Auntie winked.

"At least it got you a mansion in Beverly Hills," I said, trying to console myself.

Auntie nudged me conspiratorially. "A friend lets me use her address, kiddo. That's to fool the producers. If they knew I really lived in a cheap studio apartment, I'd never even get bit parts."

"How could you afford all those treats for my family?" I asked.

She flattened her palm against the sofa-bed. "Sometimes I was able to call in favors from friends. Most of the time I used my charge card."

I thought of all the times she had bought meals for us at fancy restaurants. "Your card must be maxed out by now."

"Don't you worry about your auntie," she reassured me. "I got an angle for everything."

Suddenly I felt angry at all those stupid producers who would ignore such a talent. "Well, all those Hollywood producers are jerks. But it'll be okay. Talent will win out, and those studios will realize what they're missing. You're going to have those producers beating down your door to have you do films."

"I like your spirit, kiddo. We'll get that movie made somehow." She laughed.

I couldn't let her go now, knowing what I did about

her life. "If you're having trouble, Auntie, we'd be glad to help you out. And you're a natural at publicity. A business up here would do well."

"I always manage." She looked as nervous as a little kid who had broken a window. "By the way, I'd appreciate it if you didn't mention this conversation to anyone else, kiddo—especially your mom. She doesn't have your . . . um . . . savvy about my playing the angles."

It seemed strange to be protecting Mom, but I nodded my head. "It'll be our secret."

Auntie and I sat staring at one another for a long while, and then Auntie scratched the tip of her nose. "Funny. I don't know what to do now. By this time, the director usually shouted, 'Cut.' "

I think we were both relieved when we heard Mom's knock. "Auntie? You have a guest."

"In a moment," Auntie muttered hastily, trying to repair the damage her tears had done.

Mom didn't have any more luck hearing her than I had, because she opened the door. "It's Linda to see you. Oh, hello, Lily."

"I don't know if you remember, but you said you knew the name of a lawyer who could help my mother?" Linda said to Auntie.

"Of course," Auntie said.

Linda was usually so calm and collected in school that it was a shock to see her so agitated. "Lily," Mom said, and motioned for me to leave.

"No, it's all right," Linda said. When Mom had

121

closed the door, Linda asked me, "Lily, how are you?"

I made room for her on the sofa-bed. "You know about the attack?"

Linda nodded. "You know Chinatown. The gossip's all over about how you were attacked at the restaurant."

"Yeah, kind of crazy. Did you hear about the Wongs?"

Her voice became tense. "The theft's all over Chinatown too. I know that I'm supposed to admire her courage in defying the Powell Street Boys, but I think that if she can afford expensive things like the Goblin Pearls, she can pay her workers. My mother says the Wongs will make things okay tomorrow. But I thought I should get the name of the lawyer, just in case."

"Why does your mom expect to get paid tomorrow?" Auntie asked.

"Mr. Wong told her this afternoon," Linda said. "The foreman called her into the office to talk to him on the phone."

"But today's Sunday," I said innocently.

Linda smiled wryly. I don't think her mother got to enjoy many days off. "It's another rush job."

Auntie considered that. "Did Mr. Wong say where he was?"

Linda shook her head. "No, but as my mom was leaving—just before he closed the door to the office—the foreman told Mr. Wong the cigars were still here."

Auntie and I exchanged looks. So the Wongs were still around but they were in a hurry—probably to catch that plane to South America. Last night Norm had cautioned us to keep our suspicions to ourselves until the police could investigate further, but I didn't know if they had the time.

I got real excited. "Auntie, what if 'cigars' was a code word for the pearls? What if the Wongs hid them somewhere in their sweatshop?"

Auntie plucked her lip thoughtfully. "That's just what I guessed."

"What're you talking about?" Linda asked, puzzled.

"Can you keep a secret?" Auntie asked.

"Of course," Linda said.

"Even from your mother?" Auntie demanded. "It might upset the investigation if your mother let it out."

Linda hesitated. "I guess I could."

So Auntie told her about the fake pearls and our other suspicions.

Linda let her breath out in a hiss. "So all the time she pretended to be so noble, she might have been setting up the theft?"

"It's possible," Auntie said, reaching for her telephone. She tried Norm first, and when he wasn't in, she tried Officer Quan. When she got hold of him, she filled him in quickly on what Linda had said. Then she listened for a moment before hanging up in disgust.

The frustration was plain in Auntie's voice. "He didn't take me very seriously. He just said that if the Wongs were stupid enough to come back for a box of cigars, they would catch them."

I thought of poor Linda and her family, and the injustice seemed monumental. The Wongs would come out of this with a lot of money—the insurance money plus the real pearls. For a moment, I didn't even think I could breathe under the burden of that knowledge. If the police couldn't move fast enough, maybe we'd have to do it ourselves. Twisting around to Auntie, I said, "It's not fair. I don't know how much we might be able to do, but we ought to at least try to help Linda. Maybe we can even find those pearls and prove the Wongs are crooks. Then her family could get some of the money that's owed them."

Auntie put a hand on my shoulder. "Wait a moment. Isn't it enough you were attacked last night? Why go looking for trouble? Let's let the police handle it."

Linda shook her head. "It's not your problem. I just want the name of that lawyer."

"It's not like Tiger Lil just to give up," I argued. "Remember *Hold That Tiger Lil*? When the bad guys were closing in, and the only way out was to make a big leap across the alley?" I spread out my arms as I fed her a key line from *Hold That Tiger Lil*. "Come on: 'What the heck?'"

Auntie's eyes crinkled as she smiled at the memory; but the corners of her mouth couldn't stay up. As they drooped into a frown, Auntie sighed. "That was just a movie, kiddo. I was just acting a part, and I had a script. I knew how things would end. I don't have a script on my life."

I dug an elbow into her ribs. "You told me that some of the best lines in your movies were your own ad libs. So you don't really need a script." I wished I could take all the love I felt for Auntie and pour it into her. "You can do anything, Auntie."

Auntie snapped her usual wisecracking mask back into place as she picked up a used Kleenex and balled it up inside her fist. "You ought to be a film director. You almost got me believing I can do it."

"You said we were all Chinatown girls." She had implied that there was a bond linking us three. And even if I didn't want that connection, she had hinted that it was part of me.

Auntie pointedly ignored me as she picked up her little address book. "Now, Linda, don't get thrown off by the fancy name of this outfit. This guy's an old hippie who got into law."

So much for the courage and determination that I had seen in her movies. For one bitter instant, I thought that I had been stupid to think a Chinese American could have all those things. And I resented Auntie for fooling me into thinking that.

"Don't be a coward, Auntie," I scolded.

Auntie spoke to Linda rather than to me as she began copying down a phone number onto a pad. "You'll have to forgive me if Lily and I try to stay out of trouble."

Linda still looked miserable and uncertain as she took it. "Thank you."

I couldn't stay mad at Auntie for long, though. After a moment's thought, I couldn't blame Auntie. Her ego had taken a pretty bad beating this weekend. And yet I couldn't help feeling sorry for Linda. "Linda, I'll see you to the door."

As she clutched the paper in her hand, Linda walked down the hallway in a daze.

I kept pace beside her, ready to keep her from bumping into a wall in her state. "So are you going to call Auntie's lawyer friend?"

Linda drew the paper through her fingers nervously. "Would her friend listen to just me? Wouldn't Mother have to be the one to file a complaint?"

"In the meantime, the pearls are probably right there in the shop somewhere," I grumbled, feeling helpless.

"They might as well be on the moon." Linda fluttered the sheet in the direction of the sky.

Helplessness quickly changed to anger. All my life, I had sat on the sidelines while the game got played. I couldn't hang back anymore. I could no more walk away from her than I could have walked away from the victims of a train accident. I couldn't do anything about their lives in the projects, or lawsuits or court cases, but I could try to find the pearls and stop the Wongs.

Even if Auntie wasn't going to live up to her name, I would. For someone in the family, Tiger Lil had been more than a role, more than a job.

"Let's get the pearls," I suggested. "Maybe the insurance company will give a reward, or they can be sold once the Wongs are in jail. Then there'll be money to pay the workers. Can you get me into the shop tomorrow?"

Linda was desperate enough to grasp at any hope. "I guess so, but I think you've been watching too many of your aunt's movies."

"Maybe," I confessed, "but wouldn't you rather have some hope than none at all?"

She glanced at the list. "Yes," she admitted, and then more strongly, "yes." Suddenly she hesitated. "But they don't like outsiders coming in."

"Maybe you can pretend I'm your cousin?" I urged.

She folded up the notepaper and put it into a pocket. "You're the only one I trust, Lily. You're not stuck up like a lot of the other kids. Meet me at my locker right after school."

"Thank you," I said, feeling elated. I guess she had never overheard me talking about her.

"Please be on time," she reminded me. "I can't wait around."

"What's the matter? Have you got a hot date later?" I teased.

I could never get her to crack a smile even in happier, less tense times. "In a way," she said with her usual aloof manner. "Just be there, please."

She started down the stairs and turned around by the front door. "Thank you," she said.

"No, thank you," I said, and meant it.

When I went to school Monday, it was still drizzling; and even in school the air felt damp and clammy. I walked down the hallways of Morris Sachs doubly nervous. Not only had I promised to find the pearls with Linda, but I had to face Barry, who had witnessed my humiliation at the parade.

He was waiting with my other teammates in the computer lab. Akeem nodded to me excitedly. "Did you see the nerd in your great-aunt's jar?"

Ariadne laughed. "He was hilarious, wasn't he?"

I didn't dare look at Barry as I waited for him to tell the truth and shrivel what little reputation I had.

"Oh, I don't know," Barry mumbled without glancing at me. "I think you ought to give him some credit for trying."

"But he almost demolished the last half of the parade," Akeem protested.

Barry answered in a voice that was barely above a

whisper. "But you remember the product. And isn't that the name of the game? Pretty clever of your great-aunt, I'd say." And he winked at me.

He was giving Auntie and me both more credit than we were due. "It wasn't planned," I confessed.

"You can't tell me that wasn't a professional stuntman," Barry whispered.

Ariadne had leaned forward to hear Barry better. Now she straightened up excitedly and turned to me. "Was it?"

"You can't expect Lily to give away all of her great-aunt's secrets," Barry muttered, turning back to the monitor.

The rest of the day seemed to take forever, and my mind was only half on my classes, so a couple of times I got reprimanded. For the last couple of classes, I carried around my book bag with all the stuff I would need. That way, when the school bell finally rang, I could go straight to Linda's locker.

However, when I saw Barry, I snagged his arm and stopped. "Thanks," I panted.

Barry's eyes flicked desperately from side to side as if he wished Akeem were here to use as his mouthpiece. In the end, though, he was reduced to whispering an uncertain, "Forget it. W-w-want to get a Coke?"

I remembered Linda, though. "Some other time, okay?"

Poor Barry had no ego at all. "Sure."

I wanted to reassure him, but Linda had made a

point of being on time. "We'll talk tomorrow," I promised, starting to jog down the hall.

Linda was waiting beside her locker with a book bag filled with twice as many books as mine.

She was even more serious and subdued than usual, as if she were already regretting her bargain with me.

From school, we headed silently down the hill into Chinatown. The drizzle had stopped, but the streets were still wet. Overhead the clouds were black, and the air felt warm and heavy with rain.

In the distance somewhere I heard the rumble of thunder, but as yet there was no relieving rain, just that steady drizzle. The discomfort made me want to scratch all over. But since I could hardly do that in public, I almost wanted to whine with frustration.

The farther we plodded down the hill, the thicker the air felt, until it almost seemed like water. With increasing excitement, I watched the green-roofed buildings slowly grow larger like giant, arched lily pads. I went into Chinatown proper several times a week, but only to buy stuff. In fact, I couldn't have told you much more about the town than any Idaho tourist—maybe less if the Idaho tourist had taken a professionally led tour.

At St. Mary's, which was Catholic, you could see the grandparents waiting to pick up their grandchildren and take them home to baby-sit while the parents worked. Other kids were playing on the asphalt basketball court in back of the school, their voices booming

130

hollowly up the rotunda. They would attend the Chinese-language evening school.

Mom and Dad had made Chris go for four years for a formal education before he rebelled. I remember the blowup, and it had been such an unpleasant time that Mom had backed off on me. So it had just been Dad who had tried to make me go, but I had managed to get around him—though he had warned me I would be sorry. And in fact, Chris had gone back in high school to learn Chinese.

As we headed into the old part of Chinatown, I began to think that this was going to be one of those times when Dad was right. I understood Chinese better than I spoke it—I could talk only in broken Chinese and had to censor myself as I spoke so I wouldn't use the swear words I heard in the streets.

Linda and I passed by the old store that, fifty years ago, used to broadcast its own weekly hour of Chinese music and news. Auntie had gotten her first taste of show biz by imitating a singer called Ethel Merman, belting out Broadway showstoppers in Chinese. In my mother's time, it been converted to a little diner where the school kids had hung out. And now it was a souvenir store specializing in toys from Japanese animation, or anime.

There were all these layers to Chinatown. The map that Auntie would have drawn was different from any my mother would make and far different from my own; and yet they all fit together like the levels of an ancient city.

The old, dark brick buildings squeezed against one another and the street, making the streets themselves appear so dim and narrow that the fire escapes on either side of the street seemed to cage the sidewalks. Chris called it "deep Chinatown"—the heart of Chinese America. Now I was going to see it with the eyes of someone who lived there.

Linda turned into an alley where the asphalt had worn away in patches, revealing cobblestones. She seemed to grow more nervous with each step as we passed building after building. There were apartments upstairs; downstairs, what had been stores now had sheets and curtains hung in the windows so you couldn't see inside.

Linda paused by an orange-painted storefront. "You swear you won't tell anyone what you see?" she asked.

That wasn't exactly what I had promised, but I had come this close. "I ask you before I tell."

She gave a hitch to the book bag hanging down her back. "I trust you." Turning, she pressed a buzzer. A moment later the door cracked open a fraction, and I saw an eyeball scrutinizing us. Within, the massed hum of sewing machines muffled a loud Cantonese song. In the snatches I heard, the woman was singing about an unrequited love. The tune, though, sounded familiar, and I realized it was a translation of "Your Cheating Heart."

"How've you been eating, Uncle?" Linda asked in greeting.

"Who's that?" the eyeball growled.

I was worried at first, but Linda explained, "My cousin. She's just moved here." I assumed that the "uncle" was an honorific rather than a real blood tie, because Linda spoke Toisanese like my parents did, while the eyeball spoke in the dialect of the three districts around Canton. (Chris had told me that Toisan was a subdialect of the four districts dialect. Most Chinese Americans came from Toisan.)

The eyeball gave a grunt and disappeared. A moment later, I heard a chain being drawn back and the door was opened. I followed quickly on Linda's heels before anyone could change their minds.

The eyeball, it turned out, belonged to a little man with a sagging face. His jowls sagged with his chin, and there were pouches under his eyes, so even his eyes seemed to be drooping. He wore a knit vest over a plaid flannel shirt. There were odd bulges under the vest where the shirt pocket would be, so I assumed that he had some pens. His legs were encased in elephantine tan work pants over sturdy, sensible shoes. From the way he acted, I figured he was the foreman.

"Mama," Linda shouted over the music and the machines, "look who's come to visit. It's our cousin."

I had passed by sweatshops all my life, but it was the first time I'd ever been in one. Light bulbs hung down from the ceiling, but there weren't enough, so it was dim inside there, and stuffy too. I couldn't have read there, let alone sewed. Ringing the room were wheeled iron clothing racks bulging with clothes. There was a space between two racks, and through it I saw a door labeled "Office." In a space between two other racks, I saw an open door leading to the solitary toilet.

Five tables had been set up, with four sewing machines on each table. At each machine but one sat a woman. Every woman wore a short cotton apron with pockets. Some wore floral patterns and others had animal prints. And at each station were piled stacks of cloth cut into triangles and trapezoids. In hampers at either end of each table, I saw more piles of cloth pieces. The women were busy assembling the pieces like jigsaw puzzles into lovely, lacy blouses. Some of the finished ones lay behind the sewing machines. An old lady in a ghastly orange knit tam-o'-shanter went around picking them up and hanging them on the racks.

At a table all the way at the back, a woman looked up. She seemed like a shorter, older version of Linda, but her hair was cut short, almost like a bowl. "Tell your cousin to come here," Mrs. Chin called without stopping what she was doing. It was almost as if her fingers had eyes.

As we made our way in the narrow aisle between racks and hampers, I could see the other women glancing at me from the corners of their eyes, though they did not stop stitching the pieces together.

Mrs. Chin's neighbor went on sewing a sleeve together. "Where are you from?" she asked me. "Did you just come over from the Middle Kingdom?"

This is the moment I had been dreading—having to use my broken Chinese. I tried to keep my reply short. "No."

A woman from the row in front glanced at me over her shoulder. She wore an apron with pandas on it. Though she went back to her sewing right away, I didn't doubt that she had taken a mental photograph of me. "Hong Kong then," she asked, trying to place my accent.

I knew that with my broken Chinese, I could never pass for a Just Off the Jet, and knowing that the suspicious foreman was eavesdropping, I said, "I come Seattle."

"Ah," the panda lady said, "native born." From the way she said it, she didn't mean it as a compliment.

A woman from the opposite end of the table called, "I didn't know you had relatives in Seattle, Mrs. Chin."

Mrs. Chin looked at her daughter puzzled, as if she wondered what the game was, but she said, "Yes, we do, Mrs. Lee. Distant relatives." She added a Chinese phrase that I did not recognize but I assumed it was my specific kinship. There's a Chinese term for almost every part of the family tree. Auntie said if you wrote all of them down, you'd have a book the size of a telephone directory.

The panda lady began attaching the sleeve to the torso of the blouse. "I know some Chins from Seattle. They own a janitorial service."

"I not know them," I said, and shook my head for emphasis though she couldn't see me.

The panda lady, though, wasn't going to take no for an answer. "You must know them. They're very prominent in the Chin family association."

Mrs. Chin came to my rescue, though. "They don't go down to the Chinatown there, Mrs. Fong. Her mother often complains in her letters."

"Ah." Mrs. Fong sighed and shook her head. "Native born." She still didn't think it was praise. "You should spend time learning Chinese, not English."

"You have to learn English to get ahead," Mrs. Chin defended me. "Or you'll be stuck here all your life."

"I learned English but I'm still here," Mrs. Lee called from her station, and then said to the woman in the ugly tam-o'-shanter, "I need more shoulder pieces."

With a nod of her head, the woman in the tam bustled over toward a hamper.

"You lose the language and that's the first step toward forgetting you're Chinese," a woman at the front said.

The women in the shop debated the issue in a friendly way without losing a stitch. The conversation flowed like a current in a river, eddying for a moment while they chewed the subject thoughtfully for flavor and almost for texture, and then it moved on. But they never stopped sewing.

In the meantime, Linda made a seat for us on a big bag of scraps and cracked open a book to start her homework. Quickly she seemed to shut out the whine of the machines and the loud, syrupy music so she could lose herself in the cool, abstract playground of mathematics. I would've tried, but I could barely read in that dim light; and besides, I wanted to watch and observe. From the way Mrs. Chin coughed and breathed, though, I knew she must be ill. If it had been me, I would have called in sick.

Leaning close to Linda, I whispered, "Shouldn't your mother be home?"

Linda seemed amused as she looked up from her math book, and she angled close to me, her breath tickling my ear as she whispered back, "She won't get paid if she doesn't work. There aren't any health benefits here and no sick leave."

I shook my head at the injustice of it all. At that moment, though, Mrs. Chin finished assembling all the pieces. The blouse looked very elegant and expensive. I bet anything it would cost eighty dollars in one of the fancy stores downtown. "There's fifty cents," she announced with satisfaction, and put it behind her sewing machine for retrieval.

When I looked at Linda, puzzled, Linda whispered to me, "She gets paid by the piece. The price varies by the item. Today it's fifty cents for a blouse. Some of the biggest clothing designers contract with the Wongs to have their clothing sewn here." She nodded to the hamper. "They have the fabric cut and send the pieces here to be assembled."

"How much is it by the hour?" I asked Linda.

"My mom's a good sewer and she works hard, but

she's never made more than minimum wage," Linda explained. "Even though she works ten to twelve hours a day and six to seven days a week, we can barely make ends meet."

I bet the Wongs were getting more than fifty cents for each assembled blouse. If I had felt it was unjust before, I felt almost physically sick now. "That's not fair."

"They owe all the women three months' wages. They keep promising to pay them, but then they keep putting them off. Only what can you do?" Linda asked, and lost herself again in her textbook.

Well, I'd catch those Wongs for fraud, for one thing, and get that money for the women. And for another, I'd definitely write an article about all this and make sure it got published. And I started writing down notes—I just hoped I could read later what I had written down half blind. When I had read about the factories in Charles Dickens, I had figured that those conditions were in the past. I never expected to find them right under my nose.

At about three o'clock, a group of five children of various ages came into the sweatshop. Two of them trooped to the back of the shop to greet Mrs. Chin. The others went to other women in the shop.

Linda leaned her head next to mine. "Remember your promise," Linda whispered to me. "You won't tell anyone about what I do."

I was careful to keep my voice just as low. "I don't see anything to be ashamed of."

Linda gave me a timid smile. "The kids at school just wouldn't understand."

I didn't see what she was afraid of revealing. If anything, it was me and the other kids who ought to be embarrassed for misunderstanding her so badly. However, before I could tell her, Mrs. Chin was waving a hand at us.

"Say hello to your cousin," Mrs. Chin instructed the boy and girl.

The little girl regarded me curiously. "But we don't have a cousin."

"We just never talked about her," Linda said. "She's from Seattle. Now do your homework."

When Linda called the other three, they came to the corner, where each of the children assumed a place on the floor as if that were his or her particular spot. A couple of the boys seemed bored, but Linda coaxed them into studying. When she was sure they had all settled in, she began her own assignments again. Suddenly I understood why she had no time for outside activities—or why she never had money for the little pleasures the rest of us took for granted. She was busy running her own little day-care center. That wouldn't give her much time to entertain, either.

In comparison to Linda, I felt like a lazy, spoiled slob. "Linda," I said.

"What?" She looked up impatiently, hating to be taken away from her lovely world of mathematics.

How could I tell her that I had misjudged her? She

took such pains to keep her life secret from everyone at school. I swallowed my words. "Nothing," I grunted. As Linda went back to work, I promised myself that I would be a much better friend to her from now on.

The foreman had been watching the room like a prison warden. Walking up and down the aisles, he would tell someone to be more careful or someone else to hurry it up. All the while he kept sipping tea from a thermos with a spigot. I figured he must have a bladder the size of Montana.

Finally, though, even Superman had to visit the little boys' room. As soon as he shut the door, I yawned and stretched. "I stiff," I said to no one in particular.

I pretended to work the kinks out of my legs by strolling up one side of the sweatshop. When I came to the office door, I glanced behind me. Everyone was busy sewing and the foreman was still away.

Taking a breath, I tried the doorknob and found it wasn't locked. But it didn't have to be, I reasoned—not with the women at their sewing machines all the time and the foreman keeping watch.

I opened the door and slipped inside. There was a desk against one wall that seemed a jumble of pastel papers—pink second pages and yellow third pages and so on. Filing cabinets filled one wall, and boxes a third. Over the desk hung a cotton blouse dyed bright purple and decorated with hundreds of orange beads in a floral pattern. But nowhere did I see a safe where someone would keep priceless pearls.

I was just about to go into the room and start look-ing in the filing cabinets when I felt a damp hand grasp my shoulder. "What're you doing in here, girl?" the fore-man demanded.

"I . . . I call home," I stammered, and pointed at the telephone for emphasis.

His face was a study in righteous indignation. "To Seattle?"

In the corner, Linda and Mrs. Chin looked as if they had been punched in their stomachs. They were proba-bly worried about Mrs. Chin losing her job. I was trying to figure out another alibi when I felt someone slap me on the side of the head. It was like the movie slaps Auntie had once demonstrated to me, which sounded and looked painful but were actually painless.

"You stupid girl," the woman in the orange tam-o'-shanter scolded. "You call your boyfriend on the pay telephone outside." She reached her hand back and gave me a slap that sounded loud but felt as light as a pat.

As I pretended to rub my cheek, I studied the woman closer. Beneath the makeup and the hat and the loud polyester blouse and pants was Auntie Tiger Lil. She winked at me. She must have remembered the name of the sweatshop and looked up the address. I should have known she wouldn't let down another Chinatown girl like Linda—even if she had no script and was forced to improvise.

She'd just been trying to keep us away from danger.

I did my best to put on a sullen, desperate expression. "My grandfather worry. I got call now."

Auntie gave a nod of approval at my acting and then in a loud voice announced, "Liar."

And then she guided me away from the stunned foreman with a flurry of slaps and punches that hurt no more than a butterfly's wings.

# CHAPTER FIFTEEN

"Please," Mrs. Chin begged Auntie, "she didn't mean any harm." She started to rise in alarm from her machine.

"Well, you've learned your lesson, haven't you?" Auntie demanded. "You won't go anywhere where you're not wanted, will you?"

I played along with Auntie. "No, I not," I whimpered, and even managed a sob for effect.

The foreman looked like he was considering evicting me anyway; but at that moment someone banged at the door. The foreman stormed angrily toward the door, and as soon as he peeked out, he changed magically. "Mr. Wong, Mrs. Wong, come in. Come in." Beaming broadly, he opened the door and backed away.

Auntie pulled her tam lower on her forehead and bent a little more to hide her face. She gave me a little shove on the hip toward the corner, and I retreated toward Linda.

Plopping down, I hid my face in my book. When no one called out that I was an impostor, I risked glancing up and saw the Wongs making their regal progress into the room.

Mr. Wong had a fleshy face with thick lips. In a way, he reminded me of a bull. Or at least he had the face of a man who was used to getting what he wanted.

As I watched, he unzipped his blue coveralls down from his collar to ease the pressure on his thick neck. Beneath the coveralls were the lapels of an expensive suit. Despite the costly clothes, I shivered. His shape was about right for the thief and for the man who had attacked me at the restaurant. I tried to shrink behind Auntie, hoping that he wouldn't see me.

Mrs. Wong was also wearing blue coveralls, on the back of which was stenciled the name of a designer label. And her bouffant hairdo had been pressed inside a cap— which she now took it off so she could fuss with her hair.

The foreman pointed significantly at the office door. "Madam, there's a mirror in my office." The funny thing was that I couldn't remember any mirror on the wall, but maybe there had been some small hand mirror in there that I had missed.

With a nod to her husband, Mrs. Wong went into the office. "Look studious," Auntie whispered to me while she began to busy herself about the shop.

I sat down, bending my head over my book but keeping an eye on Mr. Wong.

The foreman dipped his hand beneath his vest.

"Cigar, sir?" He produced two of them from his shirt pocket, and I realized what I had thought were pens were actually cigars.

Mr. Wong examined the cigar with a frown, as if it wasn't the quality he was used to; but he resignedly bit off one end and spat it out. "How's it been going today?"

"Very good, sir," the foreman said as he took out a cheap little plastic lighter. "Even though one machine is broken, we've kept up the quota."

Mr. Wong leaned forward and lit his cigar from the lighter. After a few experimental puffs, he scowled as if the cigar were even worse than he had anticipated. "Then what's she doing here?" He used the cigar to indicate Auntie, who was industriously hanging up completed blouses.

The foreman lit his own cigar. "She begged so much for some kind of work that the other women felt sorry for her. So they're each putting in a nickel from their own pockets to let her have a dollar. That way she can buy some food."

Mr. Wong puffed away at his cigar like a locomotive on overtime as he did the figures. "Who's putting in the other nickel?"

The foreman took out his cigar. "Well, I thought—" he began.

"You thought wrong," Mr. Wong said from around the side of his mouth. "The nickel comes out of your pocket. I don't have any dead wood in my shop."

For a moment, an expression of rage flashed across

145

the foreman's face, but he quickly masked it. His hand shaking, he took a couple of puffs from his cigar to calm down before he spoke. "With all due respect, sir, I have not been paid in three months."

Irritated, Mr. Wong rocked up and down on the balls of his feet. "You will be, you will be."

All around the shop, the machines had slowed as the women eavesdropped upon the exchange, and they looked back at Mrs. Chin every now and then. Now the machines stopped altogether, and each woman turned to Mrs. Chin.

Nervously she stood up and smoothed her apron. "Excuse me, sir," she said.

"Get back to work," Mr. Wong snapped.

Mrs. Chin hesitated, her knees starting to bend automatically, but she caught herself. Instead of sitting down, she left her stool and went toward Mr. Wong. "It's been a long time. Can you tell us when we'll be paid? You promised."

Mr. Wong's eyes flicked toward his foreman, but for once his foreman was in sympathy with the women. He wouldn't have minded knowing when he would be paid as well. "You'll all get your money," he growled. "My enemies have spread lies about me."

Mrs. Chin swallowed. "Perhaps first you wouldn't mind telling me why you're wearing those clothes. Are you hiding from someone?"

Probably from the police, but I couldn't say that without giving myself away.

"Can't I dress the way I want in my own shop?" He glowered. "You're fired."

Beside me, Linda gave a gasp, and her mother flinched. She held her ground, though. "Then with all due respect, sir, I would like to be paid my back wages right now."

No one said a word. No one moved. There was only the droning of a tenor for his lost love. Suddenly Mrs. Wong waltzed out of the office. Her hair was still a mess, as if she had not found a mirror; but it didn't matter, since she had put the cap back on her head. In her other hand, she had the loud, ugly blouse. It was funny that she should be taking that particular one. To her husband she announced, "I suppose we should take along some of these other blouses so no one will get suspicious."

Hooking the hanger with the ugly blouse onto a rack, she began to tuck her hair back under her cap.

"Suspicious about what, Mrs. Wong?" the foreman asked. "And who? Your husband told us the stories were just lies, and you were innocent." There was an edge rather than a deference to his voice. "That's why I helped you with the 'cigars.'"

Mrs. Chin thrust her hand out. "I want my money now."

I thought I saw sweat beading Mr. Wong's forehead. "All right, here." He made his biggest mistake when he reached for his wallet.

Mrs. Fong shot up from her stool. "I want my money too."

147

"And me," shouted another woman.

"Me too," a third woman said. She rose so hastily that she knocked over her stool.

All over the room, women were getting up and surging toward the Wongs desperately. I suppose they were thinking of their families, who were depending on the money.

Mrs. Wong dropped her cap. "Get back." She shoved at the nearest woman; but the seamstresses were in a panic now. Three months of back wages might mean the difference between life and death to their families. Surrounding the Wongs with outthrust hands, the sweatshop women backed the owners and the foreman up against the racks.

"Give us our money, Wong," they shouted.

Mrs. Wong shoved and slapped, but they only shoved and hit back. "I'll call the police," the foreman shouted to Mr. Wong as he started to push his way through the women.

For the first time, I heard real panic in Mr. Wong's voice. "No, no police," he yelled. I suppose he didn't want the police questioning him about the pearls or his whereabouts on the night of the parade.

The foreman whirled around. "Why not?" he demanded sharply. "Are your enemies' stories true?"

"I'd rather take care of it." Turning to the women, he began pulling money from his wallet and throwing it at them. "Here, here."

In their fear, the women started to fight one another

to snatch at the bills. A couple of them tumbled backward against a table. A sewing machine crashed to the floor. A half dozen women surrounded the Wongs demanding their full pay.

Mrs. Wong shouted at them, but in all the commotion, she couldn't make herself heard. In the corner, the children huddled against Linda, who put her arms around as many as she could reach. I took the opportunity to drift over to Auntie.

It was so noisy now that there was no way the Wongs could overhear us. "Why didn't you tell me what you were really going to do?"

Auntie adjusted her tam. "If I had told you what I really had planned, you would have insisted on coming along. And the Wongs had already attacked you once, kiddo. I didn't want to risk it."

I felt awful for what I had said to Auntie last night. Coward indeed! "I should have known you were only acting. You really are Tiger Lil."

"That may not be as much of a compliment as you think." Auntie chuckled. "There are some critics in Hollywood who would have said that I never acted: I only played myself." Auntie nodded to the storm swirling around the Wongs. "But maybe you ought to leave, kiddo."

I shifted my feet slightly to get a better view of the Wongs, and from the side of my mouth I explained, "You said that all the women in our family have a stubborn streak—well, that includes me."

"Some would call it a streak of stupidity," she muttered, but she winked at me approvingly.

"How did you get in here?" I asked Auntie.

Auntie sadly watched the riot. "I waited outside until I saw a woman starting to go in. She was happy to let me take her place today for a hundred bucks."

So would I if I hadn't been paid in months. As I watched the women fight the Wongs, I said, "I didn't know you could sew."

"I couldn't sew a stitch to save my life. That's why God invented wardrobe people." She chuckled again. "I just sabotaged the particular machine I was assigned to. Then I begged the foreman to let me hang around and do odd jobs. A day's work for a whole buck. The mean son-of-a-gun wasn't going to even let me do that, but the other women said they'd each chip in a nickel if Mr. Wong would."

"We'll have to do what we can for them then," I said sadly.

"Yes," Auntie agreed.

I leaned against the clothing rack. "Did you find the stuff?"

Auntie glanced toward the Wongs, but they were still involved in the riot. "I got a broom and swept up, so I got all around in here, but the foreman got real nervous when I tried to go into the office. So I waited until he was occupied in the W. C."

"And?" I asked.

Auntie shook her head. "Nothing."

I kicked at a scrap of cloth on the floor. Bits of fabric littered the floor like so many oddly shaped leaves. "You didn't do a good job sweeping."

Auntie was offended. "That floor was clean four hours ago."

Suddenly someone was banging on the door. "What's going on in there?"

I waited for the foreman to send them away, but he was just standing to the side with his arms folded thoughtfully. It was a harassed Mr. Wong who shouted, "Go away."

"Give us the rest of our money, Wong," Mrs. Fong cried.

And the other women began to take up the chant. The visitor banged again. This time he boomed in Chinese, "We know you're in there, Wong. This is the sheriff's department. We have a warrant for your arrest."

"Go away," Mr. Wong shouted frantically to both the women and the sheriff's deputies.

For all the good it did him, he might have told a cable car to leave. Something slammed against the door with a thud. Though the door was solid wood, the panels began to crack.

Startled, the women stopped and with the Wongs gaped as the deputies smashed relentlessly at the door. A moment later, the head of a sledgehammer splintered through one panel. It disappeared an instant later to be replaced by a brown hand, which found the doorknob and turned it.

When the door opened only the length of the chain, someone kicked the door so that it flew open, leaving the chain dangling from the door with its hasp.

A man in a blue jacket over his suit held up a wallet. "I'm Deputy Rodriguez. We have warrants for F. L. Wong and H. T. Wong." Beyond him there were a half dozen other men and women in blue jackets.

Deputy Rodriguez glanced around the room, focusing in on Mr. Wong. "Are you F. L. Wong?"

"I don't speak English," Mr. Wong said, which I suspected might be a lie, but perhaps his wife handled his English-speaking customers.

A Chinese American deputy followed Deputy Rodriguez into the shop. "Are you F. L. Wong?" he repeated in Cantonese. And when Mr. Wong still did not answer, he tried Mandarin.

"Call my lawyer," Mr. Wong said frantically to the foreman.

However, the foreman stayed where he was.

Deputy Rodriguez went right over to Mr. Wong, and as the Chinese American deputy translated for him, he told Mr. Wong that he was wanted for a dozen counts of fraud. And he named a number of banks as the victims.

While her husband was receiving his warrant, Mrs. Wong tried to slip around them, but a woman deputy headed over toward her and grabbed her wrist. Mr. Wong watched, dazed, as Deputy Rodriguez snapped handcuffs over his wrists.

And then after he had arrested Mrs. Wong for fraud

as well and put the handcuffs on her, he began to read them their rights.

As the police and deputies crammed into the shop, the women retreated over to our corner. "Are they going to arrest us too?" Mrs. Fong whispered to Linda.

"No, there's something about fraud against some banks," Linda interpreted for them.

Mrs. Lee whispered urgently to Mrs. Chin. "I thought it was funny how they bought so much property all over San Francisco. When you buy that much, you've got to have plenty of collateral."

Mrs. Chin twisted the hem of her short apron anxiously. "So what did they use?"

"They have that big house," a woman suggested.

Mrs. Chin shook her head. "Probably bought on a loan too."

Mrs. Fong pulled at Mrs. Chin's sleeve for her attention. "I once overheard the foreman on the phone. He said he was in charge of two hundred sewing machines, and he had the paperwork to prove it. I thought he was bragging, but maybe he wasn't."

Mrs. Chin gazed around the shop in shock and horror. "They used this shop as collateral, and when that wasn't enough, they made up figures."

"But wouldn't the banks want to see the machines?" another woman demanded.

"Not if they had forged receipts for all their machines," Mrs. Chin said. "Money gets money. If you go in like a rich person, the banks fall over themselves to give you a loan. At least that's the way I heard it worked during the real estate boom."

Mrs. Fong looked around with the same dazed look as Mrs. Chin. "I wouldn't put it past the Wongs to use the same collateral to get loans from different banks. All those buildings, all those houses and cars, and it's all built on paper."

Mrs. Chin put a hand to her mouth as a new horrifying thought occurred to her. "The banks will be first in line to take what real money there is." That was probably just twenty beat-up old sewing machines. "We'll never get our back wages." Turning, she clutched at Linda almost for support. "Come with me."

They made their way past the deputies seizing the sewing machines to Deputy Rodriguez, who was directing some of the other deputies to search the files in the office.

"Excuse me, sir," Linda said.

"Wait." Deputy Rodriguez dug a radio from the back of his belt and spoke into it. When he had restored it to his belt, he looked down at Linda. "Yes?"

"Please, sir," Linda said with as much dignity as she could muster. "When will my mother and the other women get paid? They're owed three months' salary."

The deputy sighed regretfully. "Probably after the banks get paid." He surveyed the machines being confiscated. "Which, from the looks of things, might be never."

When Linda translated for her mother, she looked

behind her at the other women. "We aren't going to get paid."

The foreman had been listening to them. Angrily he threw down his cigar. "They owe me money too." He reached for the nearest thing, which was the ugly blouse. Lifting it over his head triumphantly, he said, "So I'll take it myself."

"Leave that there," Deputy Rodriguez barked.

However, if the foreman understood English, he pretended to ignore the deputy. Whirling around, he started toward the broken door.

"Grab that man," the deputy roared, and pointed at the foreman.

A deputy coming in for another sewing machine tackled the foreman. "Let me go," the foreman shouted frantically.

"Thief," Mrs. Wong yelled. From the moment the handcuffs had closed around her wrists, she had been quiet, so the deputies had left her alone. As a result, there was no one to stop her when she threw herself at the foreman. "How dare you." Grabbing his collar, she started to shake him.

"You owe me," the foreman kept shouting over and over.

The deputy was too busy holding on to the foreman to try to fend off Mrs. Wong. Now Mr. Wong, weeping a regular river of tears, charged into the struggle. With his bound hands, he could only hammer awkwardly at the foreman's head. "Everything belongs to me. You're fired."

"Cheat, liar. I quit." The foreman began punching the Wongs with one hand.

Shouting, "Stop that," Deputy Rodriguez looked to the Chinese American deputy for a translation. Frustrated, he finally waded in himself and pulled Mr. Wong from the now-bruised foreman. As other deputies waded in, the foreman lost the ugly blouse underfoot, which seemed to make him all the more hysterical.

Meanwhile, Mrs. Fong looked around the group of women. "Well, I'm not going to let the bank take my back wages." We watched her walk over to the nearest rack and grab an armload of blouses. "And if you had any sense, you wouldn't wait around either. If you want justice, you have to seize it for yourself." And she started toward the doorway.

"The banks don't care about us," Mrs. Lee said. "Come on." Going to the same rack, she grabbed an armload for herself.

The threat of starvation made them bold. As one, the other women threw themselves at the remaining racks. Only Mrs. Chin seemed to hesitate. As she watched the other workers ripping things from the racks, she turned to Linda. "Take the children outside," she said to her, and then went to join her co-workers.

Mrs. Lee almost made it to the door before the deputies, distracted by the battle between the Wongs and their former foreman, finally noticed her. "Halt," Deputy Rodriguez shouted.

However, Mrs. Lee simply walked on into the alley.

Deputy Rodriguez grabbed the nearest deputy and shoved her after Mrs. Lee. "Get that woman."

As other women fled into the alley with armloads of expensive blouses, the deputies gave chase.

"Let's get the children out of here," Auntie said to me. As Auntie waited by the broken door, I got my and Linda's books and book bags.

Linda gathered up the children and their book bags, and we made our way past the now-empty racks. There was a small battle at the doorway between the stragglers and the deputies, but somehow we managed to squeeze by.

Outside in the alley was a plain white van that I assumed belonged to the Wongs. They had come in disguise to pretend to pick up blouses as a cover for getting the pearls. So the necklace had been in the office somewhere after all. They'd probably find them on Mrs. Wong when they finally got around to searching her.

Beyond, I saw three more vans, but these had the city symbol on their side doors. The doors were open on them all, and I saw a man in a blue derby jacket sneaking away with a sewing machine, taking advantage of the confusion. All around us, deputies were struggling with frightened workers as they sought to get the blouses.

Linda bit her lip. "Can you watch the children here? I should go back inside and help translate for my mother and the others."

"Sure, cuz," I promised.

Linda smiled at me gratefully, but as she bent to

instruct her sister, the little girl held up the ugly blouse. "Look at what I picked up. Mama will get something."

"You can't take it," Linda said, and snatched it from her. She hesitated when she saw Auntie. Impulsively she wadded up the blouse and stuffed it underneath Auntie's apron. "Here. This is in place of the dollar. I don't think you're going to get it now." She still hadn't seen through Auntie's disguise, but then I hadn't either until Auntie had slapped me—and I had lived with Auntie all these weeks. And Linda's mind was taken up with other things.

"But I'm not—" Auntie tried to tell her.

However, Linda was already hurrying back inside where a deputy had hugged her mother and lifted her, blouses and all, into the air. "Listen to Lily," she told the children over her shoulder.

Suddenly someone inside shouted, "Fire!"

"Fire," a woman shouted in Chinese.

I thought of the foreman's lit cigar rolling around in a room full of cloth scraps. Or perhaps it had been Mr. Wong's. Whoever was to blame, flames suddenly shot up among the tables.

"Everyone out," Deputy Rodriguez started yelling.

# CHAPTER SIXTEEN

Smoke poured through the open doorway now, twisting and rising like some monstrous serpent. The tables and machines sat as black silhouettes against the flames that filled the shop.

"My pearls, my pearls!" Mrs. Wong wailed as the deputies strained to keep her from reentering the sweatshop.

As the fire roared inside, I was sure I heard goblins laughing somewhere.

As we watched from a doorway, windows went up in the alley apartments and heads poked out anxiously to watch the progress of the fire. People came tumbling out of the apartments above the sweatshop. One woman was carrying an ornate clock, another a stuffed teddy bear. A third had a pair of Mickey Mouse ears.

The police were keeping people back, while the deputies confiscated the blouses from the women of the sweatshop. In a way, the women had done the designer a favor by rescuing the clothing, so the deputies contented themselves with just taking the blouses.

Mrs. Chin, her apron now sooty, came over to the doorway where we were standing with the children. I could see Linda leaning close to her ear and whispering something. Despite her ordeal, she carefully and slowly enunciated in English, "Thank you."

I suppose Linda had told her who I was.

"You're welcome," I said in Chinese, and added, "You be okay?"

Linda took her bag gratefully. "Well, Mother will have to look for work tomorrow. But we're alive, and that's the main thing." I didn't know if I could take such a positive attitude after a disaster; and it made me like her even more.

"See you in school," I said.

In the meantime, Mrs. Chin had been chatting with Auntie. "No, really," Auntie was saying, "I'll be fine. I have family who take care of me."

Mrs. Chin asked Linda for a sheet of paper, and when Linda had taken out her notebook and torn out a page, Mrs. Chin wrote down something in Chinese. "Can you read?" she asked Auntie.

"Certainly," Auntie said, and took the paper.

Mrs. Chin tapped the sheet with the pen she had borrowed from Linda. "This is our address. If you need something—a place to sleep or something to eat—you come by. It won't be fancy, but you'll be safe and comfortable."

Auntie was so moved by the offer that she hugged the surprised woman. "You're too kind."

As Auntie stepped back, I hooked my arm through hers. "She fine. She my aunt."

Linda had been staring at her while Auntie talked, but my identification was the topper. "Tiger Lil, is that really you?"

Auntie gave a little bow. "I thought I'd try and help."

"I told you about her, Mama," Linda reminded Mrs. Chin. "She's a famous actress."

Mrs. Chin looked shocked and then awed. "What's your precious name?" she asked with formal politeness.

"Tiger Lil," Auntie said.

Mrs. Chin flapped her hand. "No, your Chinese name." When Auntie told her, she got excited. "You're famous. I saw you in *Feet of Fury*." Hurriedly, she called to the other women, who crowded round. They seemed to forget their troubles when they learned who Auntie was.

"But what are you doing in that dump?" Mrs. Lee pointed at Happy Fortune.

"The same thing we are: feeding herself." Mrs. Chin nodded knowingly at the sky and then at the ground. "Whom heaven raises up, it also brings down."

"That's some fall, working all day for my nickel," Mrs. Lee muttered. "But I guess that happens to all the big stars. Didn't you save any money? Didn't you invest in any real estate?"

Mrs. Chin elbowed Mrs. Lee hard. "Now you leave Tiger Lil alone. She worked just as hard as any of us."

It sounds funny to say, but though she still kept a respectful distance from Auntie, she regarded her with an air of familiarity. I suppose she thought she knew Auntie after having seen her in several movie roles.

"Really, I'm fine," Auntie said. "I came here to try and find the pearls."

Mrs. Chin clicked her tongue. "Whatever you say, dear." It was obvious that she thought Auntie was trying to save face and had really been anxious to earn her dollar.

"I'm really fine," Auntie tried to assure her.

"Now don't be too proud," Mrs. Chin scolded her. "We'll be glad to help you. We all have to stick together."

Auntie was clearly touched by Mrs. Chin's solicitude. "You're really too kind."

Mrs. Fong pushed in next to Auntie. "Well, I don't care. Rich or poor, she was famous." She asked for an autograph, and of course everyone else wanted one too—even Mrs. Lee.

"You see? It doesn't matter what Hollywood thinks. Chinatown still remembers Tiger Lil," I whispered reassuringly to Auntie. "This is your real audience. Chinatown's still proud of you."

"They are, aren't they?" Auntie murmured. Suddenly, with a flourish, she tore the tam-o'-shanter from her head and straightened up like the inspiring star she was.

Poor Linda wound up lending Auntie her pen and then tearing most of the sheets out of her notebook as Auntie began to sign autographs for her fans. Auntie did her best to hide the fact that she was pleased.

What surprised me was how the women managed to forget their own cares for a while. Excitedly they compared autographs and stowed them away as if they had been written on sheets of gold.

Auntie capped the pen and handed it back to Linda. "Save that pen," her awed brother said.

Impulsively Auntie handed him the tam. "Here's your own souvenir." Then, as Linda's brother showed his new treasure to the others, Auntie took a deep, satisfied breath of the sooty air. "You know, kiddo, it may sound funny, but I feel like I've finally come home."

I was beginning to feel that all was right with Auntie if not with the world. "Chinatown's always been here waiting for you, Auntie."

Auntie fussed with her hair. "But I had to travel all around the globe to find it again."

At that moment, the door behind us opened. "Get out of my way, you lump of mud," a woman said. She rudely brushed Auntie from her doorstep. In either hand was a yellow-and-red plastic shopping bag filled with an odd assortment of junk. A man followed her, carrying a television set with the cord trailing behind him like a tail. I figured they were trying to save their valuables just in case the fire spread.

"It was nice to be a celebrity once again—if only for

a little while," Auntie said, but she laughed good-naturedly. And when she stepped aside to let them pass, she had recovered her old strut.

The woman with the shopping bags clicked her tongue in exasperation when she heard the sirens of a fire engine. "Now they come. I told you we left too soon."

The man grunted unhappily and shifted his grip on his television. "They aren't here yet."

The trouble was that the fire engine had to come up a narrow one-way street on which the alley opened. We could hear the driver of the fire engine pounding his horn in frustration, but there wasn't much the cars in front of him could do until the light at the intersection turned green up ahead. Once the cars had gone on, the fire engine moved past the alley, and then we heard the screech of brakes as it stopped a short distance away.

As smoke poured into the alley, firemen in black coats with yellow stripes came running in, pulling hoses behind them. Flames licked at the doorway as they stopped before it. Bracing their legs, they aimed the nozzles of their hoses and waited for the other firemen to hook up the hoses to a hydrant.

In a matter of seconds, we watched the flat hoses suddenly swell as fat as pregnant snakes, and water was gushing from the nozzles into the sweatshop. More firemen came with goggles and masks that made them seem like huge insects. As they went up to check on the apartments above the sweatshop, I saw they had tanks of air on their backs.

The women from the sweatshop watched with mixed expressions of fear for the future and sorrow, the light from the flames flickering over their faces.

"What will we do now?" Mrs. Lee sniffled. She hunted in her apron pockets for something.

"Find work first thing tomorrow." A practical Mrs. Chin fished a Kleenex from her left apron pocket and handed it to Mrs. Lee, who received it gratefully.

Mrs. Fong turned to Mrs. Lee and Mrs. Chin. "My cousin says the Prosperity Company is hiring."

"Where are they?" another woman asked.

Mrs. Fong waved her hand vaguely toward the south. "In Bernal Heights."

"So far," gasped Mrs. Lee. "We'll have to get up so early to catch the bus."

"You crossed an ocean to find work. You can cross a city too," Mrs. Chin said pragmatically. I don't think anything would faze her for long.

"Let's go together," Mrs. Lee suggested.

Eagerly the women arranged a meeting spot and time, and the kindly Mrs. Chin offered to let the other children come to her apartment in the projects, where Linda could watch them.

"Do they need a foreman too?" the foreman asked anxiously.

The women greeted him with good-natured jeers and noises, but Mrs. Chin stopped them. "They probably don't need any more dead wood," she told him. "Can you sew?"

The foreman pulled himself up straight. "Of course. My father taught me. There was a time when men did all the sewing in the sweatshops."

"Then you can come too," Mrs. Chin said. When the other women started to protest, she stilled them once again. "He's in the same boat as us, and as long as he doesn't give himself any more airs, we'll treat him as an equal."

As the firemen began to pull the blackened tables and twisted chairs from the sweatshop into the wet alley, the deputies put the Wongs into one of the vans, waiting for the street to clear. Both of them were so dazed by the catastrophe that neither of them had anything to say.

The people began to filter back into the tenement above the sweatshop with their shopping bags, and the rude woman and man returned to their apartment. One by one the women of the sweatshop said good-bye to one another and left.

The Chins were the last to go. Before they left, Mrs. Chin urged Auntie to join them the next day. When she still politely refused, Mrs. Chin shook her head sadly. "Well, don't be afraid to change your mind. Times are hard for everyone."

As the Chin family picked their way around the puddles, I took one last look at the sweatshop. "Well, wherever the pearls were, they're gone."

"And maybe the goblins too." Auntie folded her arms over her stomach and paused. "I'd forgotten all about this thing," she muttered, and poked at her apron.

"The ugly blouse," I remembered. A generous Linda had given it to her. "Why would Mrs. Wong want something like that?"

"Why indeed? I think we ought to give the blouse the once-over." Auntie jerked her head toward the street. "Let's go, kiddo."

As we made our way past the cops and deputies, I expected at any moment to be dragged over and searched; but they were too busy with their own affairs to notice one more sweatshop woman and her girl.

I didn't take a breath until we were out of the alley and back on the sidewalk near the street. I had been too busy watching the fire to see the red fire car arrive with whoever was in charge. The light on top still revolved around, sending lurid waves of red light across the building. Hoses snaked down the sidewalk from the hydrant on the corner into the alley.

"Now let's see what Mrs. Wong saw in this thing." Glancing around, Auntie pulled the blouse from under her apron and began to examine it inch by inch. "That's plastic. Plastic. Plastic." Suddenly she froze.

As I felt a raindrop touch my face, I leaned forward. "What?"

Licking her finger, she delicately rubbed at one of the beads. "Ah." With a grin, she held up the fingertip so I could see the orange dye.

"Is it . . . ?"

For an answer, Auntie adjusted her grip on the

blouse so I could see the spot where she had rubbed one bead. Underneath the dye was the iridescent sheen of a pearl. "Counterfeit plastic. Otherwise called a Goblin Pearl. The dye must be some safe, water-soluble one."

My mouth dropped open as rain pattered steadily on the sidewalks. "But she had it out in plain sight in the office."

"Where we noticed it but ignored it." Suddenly the rain began to fall in buckets, soaking Auntie, me and everyone else. The only ones who might appreciate it were the firemen. Auntie and I, though, were too enthralled to pay attention to the rain. As she spread out the blouse like a curtain, we watched the dye bleed from the pearls onto the purple fabric so that each iridescent pearl sat within a muddy brown patch.

I had to swallow a whole bunch of questions as a man passed by with a plastic shopping bag in either hand. As soon as he was out of earshot, I asked, "But why didn't the Wongs head straight for the blouse when we blew their scam?"

Auntie began to snap the pearls from the blouse and transfer them to a paper bag she had found in her pocket. "They couldn't go back because they couldn't be sure if the cops were keeping an eye on the shop. They're not too quick on their feet. They knew they couldn't go back, but they had to come up with those ridiculous disguises and set up the cover of picking up the blouses."

I chuckled. "Mrs. Wong isn't a bad actor. She had me fooled."

Auntie sniffed. "Not me," she insisted. "I can always spot an amateur."

# CHAPTER SEVENTEEN

As we sat in Norm's office late that afternoon, I felt just like the time I was sent to the principal's office—except his hadn't had a bookcase filled with law books and one volume by Stanislavski on acting. On top of the filing cabinet, Norm even had a box marked "Props" and on the hat rack was an assortment of costume hats—from a musketeer's plumed hat to a military helmet with a spike on the top. The photos on Norm's white wall were all group shots; half of them were of suited, earnest-looking lawyers and the other half were of him and other people in various costumes.

At the moment, though, Norm was definitely wearing his professional legal hat. "Well, the police lab was able to identify Mr. Wong's fingerprints among those in the women's rest room at the restaurant." He opened the paper bag we had just given him. "The Wongs were really innovative at accounting. No one's ever seen anything like it."

Auntie laced her fingers over her lap. "They should have gone to Hollywood and worked for one of the studios. The most creative people in Hollywood are in the accounting departments."

Norm began to count the pearls inside the bag. "They used the same twenty sewing machines and forged inventory lists as collateral and then hit eight banks for huge loans. And then used those loans to build a real-estate empire. There are apartments in San Francisco, condos in Hawaii. Not to mention cars, artwork, jewelry and bills from a very lavish lifestyle. It's going to take forever to untangle who gets what."

It sounded like a huge pyramid turned upside down, all resting on a tiny base that was the Chinatown sweatshop.

Auntie fiddled with the arm of her chair. "And when that started to unravel, they grabbed the chance to pull an insurance scam."

Norm put down the bag and began to examine the beads on the blouse. "It would have given them enough cash to keep the empire going."

Auntie settled back in the chair. "So they cheated everyone, including the poor women who worked in the sweatshop."

I thought again of Linda and her mother. "It doesn't seem fair," I said. "What they owed the women meant everything to them and their families, but it would only have been pocket money to the Wongs."

"Will those poor women ever get paid, Norm?" Auntie asked.

Norm rubbed the back of his neck in embarrassment. "I doubt it. By the time the banks get finished—and now the IRS is getting involved—I'm afraid the carcass will be picked clean long before the women have a turn. They're only little fish in a sea of sharks."

"Can't anything be done for them, Norm?" Auntie appealed. "To the banks and the IRS, it's just money. But to those women, it's survival."

Norm set the blouse down on his cluttered desk. "I'm afraid there's nothing I can do, Tiger Lil. Sometimes justice is truly blind."

Poor Linda. I just hoped that her mother had found a new job at the Prosperity Company by now.

"So who owns the pearls, anyway?" Auntie wondered.

"That's for the courts to decide, but I suspect they'll be sold one more time, and the proceeds will be divided among the banks and the IRS." Norm suddenly began to lay out the pearls. "Which brings me to something else. I've counted and counted, but there are only nineteen pearls here. But there should be twenty."

Auntie raised her hands fatalistically. "It's a shame. One must have gotten lost in the sweatshop before the fire."

I thought of the wall of flames. Nothing would have survived in that inferno. Even metal sewing machines would turn into strange, fused lumps. "Then it must be ashes now."

Norm studied Auntie and then seemed to make a decision. "If you ever find that twentieth one, let me know, will you, Tiger Lil?"

"What do you think I am, Norm?" Auntie demanded, the picture of outraged innocence. "Some kind of thief?"

"Then let's keep the discussion hypothetical." Norm scooped up the remaining pearls. "If a person had the twentieth pearl, what would he—or she—do with it?"

Auntie ticked the items off on her fingers. "You know yourself that those poor sewing women deserve one twentieth of the pearls. They'd get their back wages with some severance pay and a little extra for mental suffering and having to breathe the smoke from the foreman's cheap cigars."

Norm carefully poured the pearls back into the bag. "We don't tolerate vigilantes in San Francisco anymore."

Auntie agreed cautiously. "I think the police should stick to handling crime and actors should stick to acting."

His fingers pinched the small bag shut, as if closing a noose around a condemned prisoner. "Just remember: Justice may be blind, but it isn't stupid." There seemed to be some unspoken exchange going on between them, but I could not figure out what.

Finally, Auntie put her hands on the chair arms, poised to push herself up from her chair. "Well, if you don't have any further questions for me, we'll leave."

"In the future, I suggest you steer clear of crime."

Norm sighed as he put the bag with the pearls into his desk.

I didn't read between the lines until we were back outside on the sidewalk. "Norm thinks we stole the last pearl, doesn't he?"

"I prefer to think of holding it in trust for my true fans," Auntie whispered as rain began to drip off her hair. Raising her hand suddenly, she put it behind my ear and pulled out a gleaming sphere and held it before me. Even in the drizzly afternoon light, I could see the rainbows playing along its sides. It was beautiful enough to tempt goblins, let alone humans.

My jaw dropped open as the truth finally dawned on me. "Auntie!"

Auntie winked and brought her free hand up, setting a finger to her lips as uniformed police streamed out of the building. "When the Goblin Pearls are sold for the last time, the new owner will be approached—discreetly—and asked if he or she would like to complete them again."

I watched Auntie stow the pearl away in her pocket. "If Norm catches you, you're in big trouble."

"I'll risk it." Auntie patted her pocket. "After all, those women were willing to pay me out of their own pockets. And a nickel may not sound like much to someone else, but it is when you're only earning pennies."

I hooked my arm through hers, glad that she was on my side. "Who knows? Maybe it will take away the curse I heard about."

"Who knows?" Auntie agreed, as we made our way through the crowded, rainy streets to the bus stop.

The trouble was that it was rush hour, so the buses were strictly standing room only. By the time we reached home, Auntie gave a moan. "Boy, are my dogs killing me."

"Dibs on the bathtub," I said as I fished out my keys. After catching two different buses in rush hour, I felt dirty—as if half the world had rubbed against us. "I want to take a long, hot soak." Our small water heater provided only enough hot water for one real bath. Whoever was second would have to take a tepid one.

Auntie wearily dragged herself up the last step to the front door in a naked bid for pity. "Aren't you going to respect your elders, kiddo?" she asked piteously.

However, it was a performance that didn't deserve an Oscar. "Not a chance," I said as I swung the door open.

Mom's head poked out of the living room. "Thank heaven you're home." She stared when she saw Auntie in her gaudy disguise. "What on earth are you doing in that getup?"

Before Auntie could answer, Mr. Soo hurried around Mom into the hallway. He seemed so glad to see Auntie that he didn't even notice her outfit. "Where were you, Miss Leung? I've been looking all over Chinatown for you."

Auntie dumbly pressed a hand against her heart. "Me?"

Mr. Soo seized her free hand in both of his and began to pump it. "I still want you to handle all of my publicity when I move here."

I thought of Auntie's face when she had heard Mr. Soo had left the restaurant so soon. "Not so fast," I said. "Why did you run out on us at the restaurant?"

Mr. Soo was taken aback. "But you were the ones who left first. I was downstairs on the telephone telling my father back in Hong Kong what a success you had created. And when I came back upstairs, I found you were gone."

I figured Mr. Soo to be in his seventies, so that meant his father had to be in his nineties. Maybe there was something to Lion Salve after all.

"I was home all day Sunday," Auntie pointed out, taking off her hat.

Mr. Soo bowed his head apologetically. "But I had promised to go to Golden Gate Park with my great-aunt. She wanted to teach me how to skate."

Who knew how old his great-aunt was, but she definitely sounded spry. I was definitely going to have to try some Lion Salve.

"As soon as I could this morning, I started to look for you." Mr. Soo coaxed Auntie, "Please say yes."

"You're a natural at publicity," Mom urged her.

"And great at organizing events," I chimed in.

Mom wound her arm through Auntie's. "And in the meantime, I've got space at the back of my beauty parlor. You could set up a desk there."

"You must tell me yes," Mr. Soo wheedled.

Auntie feebly waved her hand in the air. "But I've got film projects."

"Can't you can work around them?" Mom asked.

"Your real fans are up here," I reminded her.

"Well . . ." Auntie said, relenting.

"What the heck?" I whispered in her ear. "Make the leap."

"Actually, kiddo, the leap was made by my stunt double, Shorty McCafferty, in a bad wig," she whispered back, and then shrugged. "But why not?"

"Wonderful!" Mr. Soo exclaimed. "I'll call you tomorrow and work out the details."

Mom was more than pleased to have Auntie staying with us. "We'll put a big sign up: 'Tiger Lil Publicity.' "

For all her virtues, Mom was never strong on imagination. "That sounds nice," Auntie said, not wanting to hurt Mom's feelings. "But under it, I'll think I'll add 'Problem Solver.' "

"A fixer," I said.

Mr. Soo said some Chinese I didn't understand.

Mom looked puzzled. "But that's a matchmaker."

"Matchmakers did more than arrange marriages, though," Mr. Soo said. "They solved problems around the village too."

Mom folded her arms. "Well, you shouldn't have trouble finding business. There's plenty of problems in Chinatown and a lot of things that need fixing."

As we escorted Mr. Soo downstairs to the door,

Auntie leaned over to whisper, "And I'm sure I'll want an assistant."

"You got it," I promised, feeling good about the future.

Once Auntie had opened the door, Mr. Soo started to open his umbrella. "I think it's stopped raining," she said, looking beyond him at the street.

Outside, the last of the clouds had drifted eastward. As far as I was concerned, the weather was perfect: the air cool and dry, and the sky, washed by the New Year's rains, a blue so bright it made me ache inside. And the whole world felt clean and new. It was a perfect time and place for beginnings.

"Aren't things splendid?" Mr. Soo enthused. Tucking his umbrella under his arm instead, he gave the thumbs up to Auntie. "Remember, tomorrow."

As we stood waving from the doorway, I suggested to Auntie, "Maybe you can even work out a movie deal with him, Auntie."

"Wouldn't that be nice," Mom murmured.

Auntie put one arm around my shoulders and her other one around Mom's. "First things first. Everyone seems so darned unorganized. I've got a few lives to tidy up."

"You're not going to retire from acting," Mom said, disappointed.

"Not even when I'm dead, kiddo," Auntie reassured Mom. "Once I pass on, I'm going to have myself freeze-dried and have myself rented out to horror movies that need a corpse." But before either of us could think of an appropriate response—if there was any—Auntie suddenly pointed in alarm at the floor. "Oh, no, Mr. Soo dropped a diamond ring."

Dropping to all fours, I searched the floor with Mom. "I'm sorry. I don't see anything," I said.

I was just in time to see Auntie scamper nimbly up the last steps to the second floor and the bathroom. At the top, Auntie laughed in triumph. "I know. I lied."

I jabbed an index finger at her in protest. "Hey, I called dibs on the bathtub."

"All's fair in love and bathrooms, kiddo." And the next instant, she had disappeared.

Puzzled, Mom said, "Now, would you mind telling me what Auntie was doing in those clothes?"

"Fixing things, Mom." I sighed, resigned to a bath of lukewarm water.

I looked around the hill and then down the street toward Chinatown. Tiger Lil was ready to jump from the silver screen to the real world. I just hoped we were all ready for her. Life was going to be very interesting with her around.

# A F T E R W O R D

Asian Americans have been involved in the movies almost since the beginning, from actors like Anna May Wong to cinematographers like James Wong Howe. In fact, Barbra Streisand coaxed the latter out of retirement to shoot her in *Hello, Dolly*. There were also singers and dancers who played night clubs and did short films as well. For a glimpse of those entertainers, you might want to see Arthur Dong's documentary *Forbidden City*.

More importantly, while Tiger Lil's career is fictional, her personality is not.